Lizzy & Darcy in Lockdown

By Joanna O'Connor

Inspired by Jane Austen's esteemed characters

Copyright © 2021 by Joanna O'Connor

All rights reserved. No part of this book may be reprinted or reproduced or utilized in any form or by any electronic, mechanical, or other means, now known or hereafter invented, including photocopying and recording, or in any information storage or retrieval system without permission in writing from the author.

This is a work of fiction. Names, characters, businesses, places, events, locales, and incidents are either the products of the author's imagination or used in a fictitious manner. Any resemblance to actual persons, living or dead, or actual events is purely coincidental.

For my beloved, beautiful,
fun-loving Mama

Dear Reader,

It's spring 1812 and Miss Elizabeth Bennet finds herself in quarantine lockdown at Hunsford Parsonage with the Collinses, resorting at last to the company, by letter, of Mr Fitzwilliam Darcy, who is likewise inadvertently incarcerated at Rosings Park with his Aunt, Lady Catherine de Bourgh, his cousin Anne, and his other cousin, Colonel Fitzwilliam.

Whilst my intention is a light and humorous glimpse into a challenging situation, I assure you that weightier matters will be addressed and respected as the letters progress.

I appreciate your presence, wish you well, and offer my felicitations.

Yours etc.

Joanna

Key

(Bracketed and written in Italics) = thoughts that are not sent.

*Referring to Mr Wickham

** Referring to Miss Caroline Bingley

***Referring to Mr Collins's offer of marriage to Lizzy

**** Lizzy is enquiring as to Darcy's involvement in Bingley's removal from Meryton, Colonel Fitzwilliam has hinted at this in his previous letter

____ Indicates a pause in the letter, while the writer collects themself.

Letter One

Tuesday 5th May, Hunsford Parsonage

Dear Mr Darcy,

I confess myself at something of a loss to explain the impropriety of my writing to you in this manner; but finding myself in lockdown after only three weeks in Hunsford with the Collinses, and having exhausted friends and relatives with repeated requests for diversion over the proceeding almost six, I must reach out to my extended acquaintance in the hopes of finding one - besides Jane - who is not already out of humour with this epidemic. Now, I give my full assurance of that being the one and only time you will hear me directly mention what is our present national - or even international - dilemma, for it does not amuse me, and - as you may remember - I dearly love a laugh.

There seems plenty, however, that surrounds the Unmentionable that *is* diverting, and - as one who is often a keen observer of the follies of others - I hope you may not object to joining me as witness to the microcosm in which we now find ourselves fixed *(or perhaps you will, in which case I really shall be none the worse)*.

My father has often referred to each of us existing within our 'own small worlds,' and in this case, he has become quite literally and figuratively correct, for my world currently consists only of Mr Collins *(whom I recently refused in marriage)*, my dear friend Charlotte *(who accepted him instead)*, Charlotte's sister Maria *(a dear girl of whom I know rather little, despite a lengthy acquaintance)*, and what missives we receive from Meryton and Rosings.

Since the National Household Isolation Edict, Mr Collins has given orders that we are all to remain separate from one another and in our rooms, with brief exceptions. Charlotte is permitted to leave hers three times a day to prepare the repast - the cook and housemaid having been hastily returned to their families - whereupon Mr Collins, wrapped in muslin, will - at a safe distance - usher her from the kitchen and deliver our food upstairs on trays. He has devised a system of miniature bell ringing, so that each may open their door to their own specific ding, thus avoiding any chance of cross-contamination. I am, naturally, infinitely tempted to open my door to Maria's tune, but have managed to resist the impulse for now. Prior to lockdown, Charlotte, it seems, had already adopted the attitude of letting her lord and master have his own way in everything, for the sake of peace - a decision, I believe, which may well fire back loudly upon her in the future *(if not already)*.

Mr Collins himself walks freely about the house *(hopefully fully clothed, although I seek no proof)*. Once a day, he dons his beekeeping attire and braves the arduous journey to Rosings, where he signals his deference to your Aunt *(Lady Catherine de Bourgh)*, and delivers written greetings to a small table you have no doubt noticed, that he carried over for just that purpose. Suffice to say he delivers far more than he receives. He would go more often, but - as you know - we are only to go out for daily exercise, to gather food, or to visit a vulnerable elderly person. By the by, if this letter seems lightly singed to you, it is because Mr Collins waves any letters - received or delivered - over a lit candle, for 'we cannot be too careful, Cousin Elizabeth.' Mr Collins, of course, keeps himself constantly informed and is even purchasing his own newspapers (also promptly singed). Consequently, he is more afraid than any other of my acquaintance. I've often reflected that we are seldom as cautious as we might be when allowing our heads to be filled with the opinions of others. A risky old business, in truth, which should be undertaken with the same prudence one might give to imbibing one of Mr Collin's home cures.

For my part, my only real fear at present is that - should we run out of provisions - we will be forced to resort to Mr Collins' potatoe patch. Such a display of unnerving forms as you have ever seen! Charlotte says it occurred owing to his planting in November during an early frost and not knowing how to chit them.

Yours etc.

P.S. Mr Collins has even tethered the village cat outside, for fear that she might be carrier. He has fashioned her a wooden collar and chain, and there she sits in a disconsolate heap, her green eyes looking up at my casement window in pleading submission.

Letter Two

Wednesday 6th May, Rosings Park

Dear Miss Bennet,

I admit myself surprised to receive your letter. But also... *(gratified...? Satisfied? No, that's worse. Flattered? Good Lord, no. Stunned...?! Gratified... Gra-ti-fi-ca-tion...)* Pleased.

(It will have to be pleased)

At present, there is little to report that may amuse from Rosings. We mostly keep to our rooms. My Aunt has *(exerted her influence)* managed to persuade three servants to remain *(at a reduced salary)*, and the Housekeeper, Mrs Norris (who I think had nowhere else to go), so at present we must make do.

It is a strange kind of independence. But not unwelcome.

(Like your letter)

The weather is unseasonably warm. Which is also... not unwelcome.

Mr Collins has skills I knew not of. I believe he has sent several homemade tonics to my Aunt. May I ask what effect they are like to have?

I trust your family is, thus far, well.

Yours etc.

P.S. With respect, potato is spelled without an e, unless you intend a plural, in which case 'es.' A common error.

P.P.S. I fear for Mr Collins once the cat goes free.

Letter Three

Thursday 7th May, Hunsford Parsonage

Dear Sir,

Thank you for your letter, and for your kind enquiry after my family. They are all quite well. My mother has placed my father under lock and key, in order to preserve his health as far as ever she may. My younger sisters *(with the exception of Lydia)* are to leave provisions for him outside his library, where a day bed has been moved. He does not consider this a hardship, and writes that he finds himself at last supremely grateful for the estate's entailment, as it allows him to read and reflect in almost uninterrupted bliss.

Mama's progress through the last few weeks has been somewhat unsteady. Her first reaction was to give a good venting to everyone, during which she rid the house of every circulating library book; something for which she now admits some remorse, for all the books in the house are now out of bounds with my merry father. My mother herself is not a great reader, but Mary considers her intellectual advancement most seriously impeded by the new restrictions.

Next, Mama set about stock piling as much food as she could, siting the Bible as reason. One of our meadows was flooded in January, then in February Kitty set fire to the hearth rug in the drawing room, so it seemed likely - with impending pestilence in March - that famine was also on the way. Jane tried at length to reason with her by letter, siting Joseph as Vizier of Egypt (Genesis 41) and paralleling his good economic sense with that of our government, but to no avail. She was not to be persuaded. Having filled the pantry with as much lardy cake and ginger wine as could be made, she is now to be found - most days - weeping in her bedroom, often joined by Mary or Kitty. Thank heavens for Jane, whose communications are all calmness and optimism; perhaps aided by the fact that she remains in London with my Aunt and Uncle Gardiner.

Aunt Phillips is the shining missive of bad news. Every family has one. She comes in state to Longbourn at least twice a week to deliver some scripted epistle of doom that floors my mother, but by which she herself is somehow completely unaffected; perhaps because she knows how much has been embellished on the way. Her good humour and dire portents make for a most confusing combination. One of her early triumphs was a note held up to the window to say that the whole neighbourhood was to be completely overwhelmed within a week by the army, home from abroad, who would dismiss the ever-popular militia to remoter climes, and then assume a power that would keep us locked inside our homes, without outdoor exercise, by any necessary force. Strict rations would be distributed door to door at an allotted time. This was later proved to be a falsehood, concocted by members of the militia themselves who it transpired had spelled official with a u. But my mother was quite beside herself.

One wonders how the government might organise the distribution of food to every household anyway, especially as most of the population was - before the Unmentionable - already mostly without it. But I am not supposed to consider these things, being a foolish female.

Ah yes, regarding your Aunt and the tonics. Mr Collin's most recent home cures have been devised upon the four elements. Thus hot, cold, dry and moist - which handily sums up the immediate reaction of the victim when consumed. His concoction of pond water, pumiced dandelion petals and pulverised mushroom wiped Charlotte out with the gripe for four days straight. Spousal duty, I imagine, for mine went instantly into a basin.

When this is at an end, I will ask Mr Collins to enlighten you on all of which he is capable.

Please remember me to Colonel Fitzwilliam, if you should see him. I imagine one might pass days in Rosings without fear of bumping into one another.

I hope her ladyship and Miss de Bourgh do tolerably well and are enjoying their prodigious fireplace and sixty-four windows.

Yours etc.

P.S. Your reply was extremely brief. But - in spite of corrections to both spelling and grammar - I am, as you can see, undeterred *(indeed, I am quite grateful for a source of near companionship)*. If you are willing then I will deliver further letters myself in the morning at 7, when the household is not yet up. Mr Collins deems my writing to you inappropriate, therefore this will be the path of least resistance. I shall be punctual; thus, you may collect from said table at five past seven without fear of either damp or impropriety. I would welcome the freedom of an early walk and will be breaking no rules as it is exercise and solitary.

P.P.S. When you speak of independence, what exactly do you mean?

Letter Four

Friday 8th May, Rosings Park

Dear Madam,

Thank you for your lengthy communication. I am most gratified to hear that your family is much as ever. I shall endeavour to fulfil your wishes and supply you with a more detailed description of my current environment; although I must first mention that, regarding Mr Collins, I would rather you did not.

I caught sight of Colonel Fitzwilliam in the breakfast room this morning, he at one end of the table and I at the other. We might have played Shuttlecock from that distance. We exchanged hasty greetings and I conveyed your good wishes to which he rejoined with his own. He seems well and as amiable as ever, though he has run out of military equipment to polish.

My Aunt and cousin take the carriage out each day for exercise and are in reasonable spirits. At least, I perceive no great difference in either. Anne fashions a new talisman for her collection every day, but again, this is nothing novel.

How-ever did you know of the sixty-four windows? I have been twice around the building this afternoon to disprove the truth of that statement, but must regretfully assent to your superior knowledge.

Do you ride, Miss Bennet? I am sure you are most welcome to take a suitable mare from the stables at Rosings should you wish. For my part, my daily rides are becoming more and more extensive and - if I do not apply due care - I will find myself back in Derbyshire before I know it, whereupon I shall no doubt receive a hefty fine and be returned by carriage to Rosings. A circumstance which might be just as well, for Pemberley is currently completely unoccupied, my sister being still confined in town and all the servants temporarily dismissed; and if left there, I would no doubt find myself soon a Timon, hunting for scraps and decrying others for the crime of being man.

You ask of my new found independence? I suspect you imply that I am at last learning to pull on my own breeches, or pull off my own boots. Is that so? I know enough of your disposition to suspect some mockery at my expense.

I have a letter this morning from one who would claim an acquaintance with you: Miss Bingley. She urges me to grow a beard, something that is now the fashion in London since we none of us may tend to our own locks. Since my independence does not yet include the easy use of a razor, I may have to regretfully comply. Mr Brummel would not be impressed. Shall I remember you to the lady, when I make my reply?

Although I appreciate that we are yet young in this occurring, I cannot help but pause to reflect upon the encouraging aspects of what is about us. The newspaper gives dire prognostications, which may be expected; but around us we may see many acts of kindness and compassion, letters filled with loving wishes, and a pause in factories, and war, while we unite in battle of another kind. What will this world be grown to, I wonder, when we emerge from this? A better one, I hope.

Yours etc.

P.S. I am willing, but cannot be so unchivalrous as to expect you to walk to Rosings in order to collect a letter by my hand. I shall therefore deliver mine at the same time, to the hollow in the old elm on the green by the Parsonage. I offer my assurance that I shall turn a blind eye to any further spelling or grammatical misdemeanours, except to respectfully mention that the 'citing' to which you refer is spelled with a c, and not an s. A common misconception. Now I am done.

P.P.S. What do you do for entertainment of an evening, when not writing *inappropriate* letters?

Letter Five

Saturday 9th May, Hunsford Parsonage

Dear Sir,

Thank you for your slightly longer epistle. I shall answer your questions briefly and in order:

a) Mr Collins is responsible for all I know of Rosings, despite my best efforts, I was bound to absorb something; b) Thank you, but I am no horsewoman; c) Yes. Both breeches *and* boots; d) Regarding Miss Bingley, no. Thank you; e) Regarding the world, I hope so too. You must remember to pay your taxes...

Mr Collins has contracted the Unmentionable. Indeed, it seems impossible that he might ever have avoided it, having thought of nothing else since its original announcement. His symptoms are thankfully only slight, but enough to take him to his bed, thus allowing the three women in his keeping to roam free. I confess, the light hurt my eyes at first and I was unsure as to what day it was, or even what month. But now I am taking the stairs two at a time, and wandering the garden openly - at a safe distance from Maria and Charlotte, of course - and the trees are all a-leaf and in blossom, and the garden at the very least in bud, if not in bloom, and I am feeling all at once the hope of spring.

Mr Collins had plans to give an Ascension missive from the top of the church tower, but for now we must postpone that pleasure, and his parishioners will be left in peace a few more weeks. I admit I admired his confidence at believing his voice might reach so far and wide, but from the plans in his study it seems he was constructing a sort of papier-mâché trumpet, which would have aided his acoustics. This, he has fondly dubbed 'the Lady Catherine,' a compliment of which your Aunt will no doubt be most sensible.

I did not know of Miss de Bourgh's collection. My sister Mary is quite vigorously superstitious too. In February, she became afraid of the colour red. Just the mention of it would send her into spasms of anxiety. Naturally, everywhere she went, red was mentioned or displayed. Now she writes that she can barely move through a doorway without performing some extensive ritual. It is no exaggeration to say that, despite these precautions, she is quite the unluckiest of people in general. In fact, I sometimes wonder whether the very rituals she employs for preservation somehow attract disaster - her focal point being unfailingly upon what she fears. Jane, on the other hand, whose focus is so very amiable and her observations always upon what is lovely and good, has few experiences that are not equally so *(with the exception of your friend Mr Bingley fleeing the county).*

Did I mention that when the quarantine edict was first issued, Mr Collins - in a heartbeat - jumped the hedge and hightailed it over two fields before he realized he had nowhere to go? For this I really cannot blame him, for it took everything in my power to resist the same impulse. Shakespeare and Goldsmith both agree - the better part of valour, is discretion, or desertion - for he did not once glance back for Charlotte. *(He who fights and runs away lives to be tedious another day...)* They say when unusual times arise, we find out what we are made of... and what those around us are made of also.

Ah yes, my evening entertainment. Prior to his confinement, Mr Collins supplied each of us with a copy of the Reverend Fordyce's 'Sermons to Young Women', two volumes, which I now enclose as loan that you may come to know him better. I must confess, it *has* amused me greatly. It is exactly the sort of book I would expect Mr Collins to have numerous copies of. Otherwise, I brought with me only three novels - none of which you might approve - and have read each several times.

But now, of course, I am a free woman. Thus, this evening I lay outside upon the front bench, with the free-cat upon my chest, and we watched the world go by in the sky above our heads. I saw the clouds tinted with sunlight move so gently across the sky, and little birds flap, flap, flap and glide. I saw Venus appear when the sky was yet quite blue, before the trees turned to silhouette and a pinkish-mauve tint brushed in pastel shades across the heavens. I saw bees and a dragonfly. The sound of bees intoxicates me.

Yours etc.

P.S. No comment.

P.P.S. I wonder, is this not a perfect opportunity for Lady Catherine to learn the pianoforte?

Letter Six

Monday 11th May, Rosings Park

Dear Madam,

I have no doubt my Aunt will indeed be delighted by Mr Collins' kind Eponym, but shall defer the pleasure of telling her till you may personally be present. Please convey my sympathies to Mr Collins, and my best wishes for his speedy recovery. If we lived in a world where all good things were possible at once, I might convey the opposite wishes to yourself and your female companions. But, alas, it is not so.

On Wednesday Lady Catherine sneezed four times in a row and is now likewise indisposed. She has - at the greatest expense - secured the resident services of an esteemed physician, who brings her meals which she refuses to *eat (and whom she alternately barks at and pleads with not to abandon her)*. I should like to tell you of her courage in the face of what is, almost certainly, a mild cold. My cousin is perhaps for the first time in her life separated from her mother, and removed to the furthest part of the house on account of her congenital delicacy.

I admit myself presently fascinated - in the face of little alternate diversion - to witness how the Unmentionable affects the people nearest to me. I observe that what was already predominantly present or inherent is merely exacerbated; thus, Anne is afeard for her health and given to emotions, yet Bingley's letters are all light-hearted affability and hopefulness, Georgiana is cautiously willing to believe in a bright future, while Miss Bingley refers mostly to the inappropriate behaviour of others and gives lengthy descriptions of quarantine vogues. Thus, with my Aunt being much as she ever was, I await her renaissance without unease. We must, however, defer her piano instruction till then.

What of Mrs Collins and Miss Lucas? You seldom mention either.

I wonder if you are not rather too hard on the regrettable Mr Collins? I am sure he must mean well, and some of his interventions have been, surely, rather inspired. Freedom aside, how do you all manage without his foraging efforts? Have you enough? A serious question.

What of your elder sister? Will she remain indefinitely in London, or are there efforts being made to bring her home?

Do you hear from any others of our acquaintance*?

Thank you for Fordyce. It shall relieve me of my current revisiting of 'The History of Little Goody Two-Shoes.' In return, please find 'A Vindication of the Rights of Woman' by Mary Wollstonecraft, which I have recently completed, and admired. May I send you anything else from my collection? You may find the 'Meditations' of Marcus Aurelius - although also not a fiction - edifying.

Yours etc.

P.S. Breeches, boots and beard! Partially. I have now wielded a razor successfully in the direction of my lower face, although am not yet confident enough of my abilities to shave about my mouth. Thus, I look - if I do say so myself - rather Shakespearean.

P.P.S. I hope all at Hunsford will accept an additional gift of what I am told is a 'pottle' of 'forced strawberries' appropriated from the Rosings Greenhouses. Mrs Norris, the Rosings Housekeeper, is a formidable lady who guards the kitchens and hot houses with the same verve with which she guards the tea, so the pottle is all I could procure for now; but I have my eye upon a ripening Pineapple.

Letter Seven

Tuesday 12th May, Hunsford Parsonage - From the Wilderness Within

Dear Mr Darcy,

Thank you for the Wollstonecraft; I have read it many times, but shall be delighted to revisit. I am familiar with Aurelius' 'Meditations,' and found them impressive, for an Emperor. I particularly enjoyed his remark 'put an end once for all to this discussion of what a good man should be, and be one.' I do like my philosophers to the point.

I doubt you will find any relief in Fordyce, but, if you should, do be sure and mark the page.

Please convey my regrets to Lady Catherine and, indeed, to Miss de Bourgh, and my good wishes for a speedy end to suffering.

I am sure you are right with regard to Mr Collins. Within our family he has seldom been thought of with any particular warmth, even before his actual person was known to us. Entailed estates do not encourage affection, you know. This might not have been unsurpassable, upon meeting, had he been a less *(conceited, pompous, narrow-minded)* silly man. I do of course appreciate that he is not without his merits - for instance, I am grateful for the origin of his postal system, and even for the singing of letters. But as to the enslaving of felines - well there, I fear, he has lost my good opinion for all time. You know how that feels*.

It therefore behoves me to tell you that Mr Collins is a most demanding patient. Charlotte is up and downstairs at all hours, warming water and making up poultices. Thankfully, she is infinitely serene. She has quite the most beautiful singing voice, the kind you might pay to hear. When she is happy, she goes to the farthest end of the garden and sings up to the sky. She might have been another Angelica Catalani. But then, who knows what may become of Charlotte yet? People have run into the night and changed their lives - why not she? Do we not all have friends we wish this for? But there are some doors which may be only opened from within.

Prior to his trial by sneezing, Mr Collins insisted that Charlotte learn a sesquipedalian a day, to improve her vocabulary *(and impress your Aunt)*. Now that he is bed ridden and 'like to die,' he has increased it to three. As he has little more than a slight temperature and a sniffle, it seems unnecessary. But ensuring that Charlotte is not left with idle hands or poor word power seems to give him peace.

Speaking of which, Mr Collins, it transpires, is a Seasonal Snooper. Charlotte has found all manner of spy glasses, telescopes and even a polemoscope in a study drawer where she had initially been seeking accounts. I am not sure the Reverend Fordyce would approve. Certainly not publicly, at least.

I am becoming something of an experimental cook. This afternoon, I made 'Honey Clouds' for which I whipped egg-whites into peaks with honey, then burnt them in a pan. They were pleasant enough 'passable, Eliza, for a gentleman's daughter' Charlotte said. Charlotte and Maria are both excellent cooks, and I begin to realise the value and independence which comes from possessing the ability to prepare a meal from scratch. I am fascinated by the sugar nips.

At present, we have plenty of milk from the three Collins goats: Evan, Tilly and Beryl. Ever practical Charlotte also makes goat's butter and goat's milk soap. We have a plentiful supply of eggs from chickens quite recklessly oblivious to lockdown.

Your strawberries were most welcome, thank you. We made Strawberry fritters and they were a decadent change from pears and apples. I would enclose the recipe, but I doubt your new found independence would yet accommodate such things. Charlotte is an excellent housekeeper, quite in her element, and has a larder filled with pickles and preserves. The only thing we might shortly lack is flour, but I hear this is a common cry at present; and of course, the harvest was so sparse last year.

By the by, I am not at all surprised to learn that Lady Catherine's Housekeeper is a formidable woman. It seems fitting. Our Housekeeper at Longbourn is disposed to nervous fits and vapours, and my father would be rid of her, if he could.

I am often most mindful of my good fortune to be out in the wilderness at this time, away from the city, with provisions enough; and every day amazed at what was once done for me without my notice. I am not afraid of it continuing much beyond this edict, but nevertheless, I am sensible at last.

Jane's account of London is cheerful enough. She remarks upon the Unmentionable only to say how much she now appreciates the shops and coffee houses and tradesmen and our freedoms prior, and looks forward to their return. If our lives are restricted in the country, theirs are much more so in town. Jane writes that they keep strictly within the house and make do. In the early stages, my Aunt and Uncle attempted to arrange for Jane's safe carriage home - indeed, Mama was clear that all were welcome at Longbourn - but it was simply not to be. The Edict was written, read, and London and all of us sealed off before anyone could make a move. Cheapside is not, however, as it may sound to you, and they will all do well there, I hope. How does your sister?

I am unused yet to this night-time quiet, coming from a house of bustle; but it is a friendly kind of silence (Mr Collins' grumbles not withstanding). I spend as much of the day as I can out-of-doors and have even taken to lying in the grass - although if you ever say so, I shall deny it. There's something that happens to one, when frequently in nature. I would describe it as a feeling of harmony or unity. Something challenging to put into words, but I feel the better for it.

The free cat now follows me almost everywhere I go, although she adamantly refuses ever to come inside the house. I have fashioned her a shelter out of wood and straw and she seems happy enough. She purrs almost constantly and licks my hand with her little rough tongue. I wonder how I shall ever leave her behind, when all this is over.

Yours etc.

P.S. I've never had a sense that I would contract the Unmentionable, even with Mr Collins in close proximity. I don't know why. That being said, I stay put. I stay put because others are afraid and they need me to stay put. I wanted you to know this *(for I cannot imagine what you will think, should you hear of Lydia's antics)*.

Letter Eight

Wednesday 13th May, Rosings Sanitorium

Dear Madam,

Thank you for your letter - a most welcome diversion to the routine of isolation.

I trust you are truly as hopeful as you seem with regard to Miss Bennet and the Gardiners? I have every confidence that they will all remain safe and sound till this has passed.

Georgiana was in excellent health, when last I heard. I thank you for your enquiry. Our residence in London is removed enough and the grounds are plentiful for exercise. I hope for the best, and would do infinitely more were it within my power.

Whatever, may I ask, is a 'Seasonal Snooper'?

Bingley once told me that both his sisters possess a wide selection of spying fans. Mrs Hurst, in fact, owns a quizzing glass through which she likes to peer. You may remember this from the Netherfield Ball last year *(how very long ago that seems)*.

Do you find you lose track of time and that days fly by?

You are likely quite right and I am beyond them yet, but Colonel Fitzwilliam has boldly declared that he is well acquainted with fritters and will cook us up a batch tomorrow night when Mrs Norris has gone to bed. Speaking of the proverbial, Cousin Anne's isolation has taken an interesting turn. She was found out - by said Housekeeper - to be hoarding large amounts of food from the dry larder within her chamber. We are under strict rationing on Lady Catherine's orders, who, like Mr Collins, is perhaps afraid we are none of us suffering enough. When confronted by said Housekeeper, my cousin bellowed 'I don't want to play the ------ pianoforte!' until Mrs Norris quailed. Anne then took four macarons and crammed them all at once into her mouth. Not a sight I thought I'd ever see, on either count. She has grown quite wild with dark imaginings, it seems, and although, naturally, I cannot entirely condone her behaviour, I may still sympathise. Mrs Norris was heard to mutter that Miss de Bourgh was 'most unladylike' and 'would have no gown left to fit her if she continued in that manner.' It may be noted, that while my cousin could do well by the gaining of weight, Mrs Norris could not. But that is most improper of me. For now, though, our Housekeeper is quite chastened and takes to her room rather early in the evening. I shall ask my cousin what she might do about the tea allocation, for Colonel Fitzwilliam grows quite fretful on just one cup a day.

I have never lain upon the grass. At least, not since early childhood. I may have to try. Is there a knack to it, or does one just lie straight down?

How is the free cat? Have you given her a name?

I sympathise with your sister. With the shopkeepers, tradesmen, warehouses and coffee houses all closed down, we may realise at last how much we owe to them. Wood Street, Milk Street, Bread Street, Honey Lane, Friday Street; I have a broader view of Cheapside, indeed of many matters, than you might realise. But perhaps you confuse me with Miss Bingley?

I never had a moment's doubt at your willingness to comply with that which gives the greatest good to all. I wonder, though, why you might believe I should?

Yours etc.

P.S. Evan?

Letter Nine

Saturday 16th May, Hunsford Feline Reformatory

Dear Sir,

Thank you for your letter and the ten sacks of flour. We now have nothing left to want.

Why, clearly a Seasonal Snooper is a person who has nurtured a tendency to peep through windows that are not their own *(all sixty-four of them)*; but rather than it being a daily habit, it is more of a weekly or monthly occurrence.

I am most thankful to hear of Miss Darcy's well-being and happy location. If one must be in London at present, those are surely quite the best surroundings in which to find oneself. I am sure she will do well there and keep in the best of health.

I have named the once-free cat Felicity, and she is currently cantankerous. Mr Collins had a gruelling night, the one before last *(or rather we did)*, but is now, it seems, over the worst. At least, he is expressing boredom and calling for amusement. He who never reads novels... Thus, he left his chamber for the first time today, and the free cat made her way up there at once and did something unmentionable, but not unpardonable, upon his pillow. As Mr Collins has no sense of natural justice *(or humour)*, she is now disgraced in chains once more. I will set her loose as soon as I may, and Charlotte has asked me to take her away with me once this is done. She is quite out of humour still about the spy glasses.

I am learning all sorts of things I thought I never should. Such as scything - beware your ankles and those of others. And the washing of clothes. What a lengthy process! We begin early and are barely done by four. Mama was always adamant that we should neither cook nor wash clothing for ourselves and, while fully comprehending her motives, I begin to wonder how I could ever have believed such dependency of value. It occurs to me that Charlotte wants so little, because she can do much for herself. Mind you, there are some tasks which she performs without a thought, that I am sure I never could.

Incidentally, Charlotte has politely asked me to refrain from any further creative cooking; she says we have not the provisions for my many mistakes. I am to follow her instructions and not to deviate. Mr Collins has attempted to reassert his authority and return us to our rooms, but to no avail. We have tasted too much liberty to let it go again without a fight.

Question: if you buy security, do you lose freedom?

With surprise, I must confess some sympathy with Miss Bingley, Mrs Hurst and their spying fans. How else may a woman ascertain the character of a new acquaintance, when she is so very limited in what she might say or do publicly?

I accept the society in which I find myself, because I must; but do not admire it much. Nor would I admire a man who attempts to raise himself, not by personal evolution, but rather at the expense of woman, reducing her to a simpering ninny that he might educate her better. Our inferiority is imposed and not inherent, thus - while society insists upon this quite ludicrous patriarchal hierarchy - we must resign ourselves to the alchemy of observation that we might better know the characters of those with whom we associate, to make the most rational decisions that we may. I look forward to a time when we all are wiser in our treatment of one another, where women are no longer 'out' upon display, paraded about with a looming expiration date of which we are all too sensible. I apologise in advance for this outburst. I do wish Mr Collins would return to bed.

I sympathise also with your cousin. With the life she has thus far led, an eruption seemed inevitable. People fear anger, their own most of all, for it is not counted as a virtue. But if you cannot admit your own frustrations, albeit briefly, privately, how may you possibly progress beyond them? Personally, I find retreating to my room, closing the door and jumping up and down repeating 'I'm right, I'm right, I'm right,' of the greatest assistance.

My cousins are fond of cricket, and I have found, too, that the whacking of a ball hard across a lawn is a great relief to any feelings of frustration. Might you and the Colonel contrive a game with Miss de Bourgh?

Yours etc.

P.S. Yes, Evan. She is a very robust goat. I thought of Fitzwilliam, but, indeed, there do seem rather many of that name already.

P.P.S. As a gentleman keenly attuned to the misconduct of others, I am half afeard of news you may have heard from home. If you know aught of any of our near acquaintance in Meryton, regarding quarantine restrictions, I would ask you to be frank with me at once. If not, accept my apologies and my silence upon the matter.

Letter Ten

Monday 18th May, Rosings Asclepion

Dear Madam,

I confess that news of your youngest sister's conduct has reached my ears. The source I will not divulge**, but as it is one to whom I would not fully give my trust, I would ask you to acquaint me with whatsoever you may wish, should you wish it.

Regarding the question of security, I am not convinced that one may purchase it at all. I am certain that freedom, as with all points of import, must be found first and foremost within oneself. Attaching one to other out of need and scarcity, rather than for a mutual, ardent and abiding love, an equal desire for participation, seems fraught with possibility for disappointment - on either side. Why do you ask?

I appreciate your 'outburst,' although I do not see it as such. Indeed, I fully comprehend your feelings and shall, if you would hear them, add my own. I believe that many of my sex are also bound, indeed, frustrated by the conventions of which you speak. While they may serve some, they most emphatically do not serve all. I might also add that while we men may experience sentiments similar, if not equal, to women, we are required to be stalwart in face of sorrow, composed in face of danger, and unflinching in each unpleasant duty. Just as you bear feelings of inequality, which I fully concede, there is much expected of my sex. Fathers, knowing this, are more rigorous with their sons than daughters, for reasons that we, as children, might not fully comprehend. I was fortunate. My father was kind.

Regarding marriage, I am fully expected to make a match which meets my own feelings last, and those of my peers first. Whilst I might truly seek an equal companion in life, the equality of rank is felt - by many - to be of far more import than equality of character. A woman of great spirit might have the most unfortunate of families, which would make the match insupportable. One with each seeming credential of good breeding may be an utter bore, having focused every effort upon superficiality and none at all on character. When engaging another for a dance, one takes a great risk. Our dances are long, and if one has made a foolish or a desperate choice, there will be an half hour to fill with idle chit chat. A skill I have no wish to acquire. I write as I think - forgive me.

If not an impertinence, may I ask what brings you happiness? I have had cause of late to consider this at length. The answer is not what once I thought.
Now, I must tell you of The Rise of Lady Catherine. I am sure it will come as no surprise to you to hear that my Aunt - formidable woman that she is - has overcome the Unmentionable, if indeed she ever had it. Twice, we were called upon to say our goodbyes. The first time, Lady Catherine lay in state, looking - I must say - alarmingly frail, having taken no repast for many days. She suffered each one of us to say what we might, then told Anne she was 'quite busting from the seams' (she is not); the Colonel that he was 'quite shockingly unkempt' (he is); and myself she affected not to recognise, but avowed that 'whoever I was' she was 'most seriously displeased with me.'

Last night, we were once more summoned, but my Aunt would neither look at nor acknowledge any one of us. Anne was quite beside herself with fearful remorse and at once set about ridding her room of any remaining provisions, asking the Colonel and I to assist her in the building of a bonfire where she might dispose of all evidence of a recent foray into archery. We agreed, reluctantly. It has been most gratifying - if a little unsettling - to see her so recently invigorated. The Colonel, especially, has been quite captivated.

This morning, quite convinced of the worst, we made our way to the breakfast room, only to find Lady Catherine ready stationed, expostulating and rapping out enough commands to right a year of wrongs. Our exclamations upon her miraculous renaissance were met with bemusement and derision. It transpires she had dismissed her physician late last night for 'gross incompetence' and 'intolerable breath,' an action with which I have much sympathy, for the man seemed far more attentive to her passing than her healing.

I confess I was greatly tempted to give my Aunt a very sound rebuke for alarming us all like that. Twice. But before I could open my mouth she said 'Nephew, if you for two moments together believed *I* could be felled by a paltry little bug like that, you are not the Fitzwilliam I thought you were.' She's right, of course, I never did believe it entirely. 'Sometimes, I like to rest and recuperate, without the fuss and bother of all of you,' she continued. 'So, I simply... withdraw.' We all have our ways. I have great affection for my Aunt - she and my mother were deeply fond of one another - and I am most relieved at her revival. I would add that, knowing she, both illness and recovery might quite justly be attributed to boredom and wilfulness in equal measure. She has ever been one to make the most of her position.

Ah yes, you speak of gardening. The gardens at Rosings are now quite overgrown, the ground staff having been dismissed long before. The Colonel and I began their maintenance recently, enlisting our cousin, who had still energy to spare. By the by, both the Colonel and I attempted to persuade Anne to join us for cricket, as you suggested, but she declined. She had developed a preference for archery, aforementioned, citing that she saw an actual use for it - whatever that means - and was quickly an accurate shot. It may please the soon-to-be-free-again cat to note, that Anne's chosen targets were a large pile of written civilities from Mr Collins to my Aunt.

Yours etc.

P.S. Another question; if you might go anywhere today, where might you go?

Letter Eleven

Wednesday 20th May, Hunsford Salon

Dear Sir,

I am most gratified to hear of your Aunt's miraculous recovery. I never doubted it would be so. I do find it in my heart, though, to hope your cousin's retreat may be short-lived. To have gained so much ground in so short a time is something of a value not to be decried.

Charlotte has at last put a stop to the newspaper, after finding Maria pouring over one in floods of tears. Thomas Gray was right, ignorance *is* bliss

Mr Collins, in his recuperating solitude, has taken up a paint brush and is endeavouring to paint each of us. He has some skill. Naturally his chief subject is your Aunt, something which may well offend his wife - although of that he will never be sensible. He has endeavoured to 'beautify' Lady Catherine, by lengthening her nose and neck, enhancing the colour of her eyes, and filling out her lips. I leave it to you to determine whether this is truly a kindness, or an affront. Although I cannot be sure whether your Aunt will notice the changes, for they are subtly done, I am quite certain that - given the right circumstances and at the earliest opportunity - Mr Collins will draw her attention to each, that she might recognise and applaud his skill. In which case, may Heaven help him.

Regarding happiness: my sister Jane. My Father, when I see him. Charlotte. Long walks outdoors (no turning about rooms for me). Having a purpose. Dancing *(even if one must suffer partners who are simply 'tolerable')*, Felicity, a good book, stimulating conversation, a curiosity satisfied *(your letters... for the most part)*, and you?

If I were free to go out, I would either take a carriage to my Aunt and Uncle and Jane in Gracechurch Street and we would go to the theatre, or I would go home to Longbourn and sit outside with my father at dusk while he smokes his pipe, and we would admire the serenity together and pour out amusements.

I am grateful to you for your description of what it is to be man. My chief experience of such is Papa, who seldom communicates such matters. I confess, though, to having had a strong inclining that we might not be *quite* as different as supposed.

You speak of a lady's family being potentially 'insupportable.' I could not marry a man who might allow himself to think so meanly of mine. *That* would be insupportable to me.

Regarding all of us, I would simply say - we have inherited this world, and only we may improve it with comprehension of what does not serve us more, and notions of what may better do. I would rather an equal partner of an unconscionable or insipid family, than an insipid partner of whom my family approves. But to each his own *(do I contradict myself?!)*.

A further wondering - what might make one lose the good opinion of a person whom one had known since childhood[*]? To whom, one might say, one owed one's allegiance? Or is it that, once grown, one now perceives a difference in rank and fortune not apparent before? That the very views that might dis-incline one from a woman of good character, on account of her 'insupportable' family, might also dim your view of friend and equal, now proven lesser by birth, though not by nature, and thus considered no longer friend?

Question: Is it possible ever to rediscover something you believe may permanently be lost?

Yours etc.

P.S. I confess, I was tempted to speak of Lydia's transgressions, but I realize now how wrong of me that is. Lydia is but fifteen. She is flighty and ebullient and trying. But she is still my sister. Your family is your family. Our loyalty to one another is of great value; not just to blood family, but to those of long acquaintance. We are alarmed that the behaviour of our nearest and dearest is a reflection upon us, and thus we are ashamed of them. But there is no love in that. I am learning that when you speak of love, you speak, truly, of appreciation. Therefore, you must attend to what you may appreciate most in one another and give all your consideration to that; their 'flaws,' and 'imperfections,' you do not see. That is much the politer way to be, do you not think? But we are afraid to show love, for fear of disappointment and rejection, and we look for flaws, that we might early save ourselves.

Perhaps you might tell me what you have heard, that I might tell you of its falsehood?

P.P.S. Regarding freedom, I could not agree with you more. It is seldom that one may have the opportunity to see, at such close quarters, the price one might have paid[***].

Letter Twelve

Thursday 21st May, Rosings Park

Dear Madam,

I believe you speak once more of the differing accounts that puzzled you exceedingly*. You ask a pertinent question. Without hesitation, I answer - one who has harmed one whom I love. I recall having once declared before you that my good opinion, once lost, was lost forever. Or something to that effect. Thus, we find our words of a moment return to haunt us; for I have often thought of what I said, and whether there was fully truth in it. But we must not quote ourselves or one another over time, for it implies an expectation that growth has not occurred.

In the case to which I suspect you specifically refer however; my feelings are unaltered. Indeed, unalterable.

Very well, I will relate in brief what I have heard of your youngest sister; but I do so most unwillingly, knowing it will cause you pain.

———

There are reports that she is 'not one to remain at home.' That she, by some - and I quote - 'self-ordained edict, in direct opposition to the one by which the rest must currently abide' - deems herself one of the few able to wander at liberty and is regularly to be seen about the town with young Mr Denny, where they endeavour to encourage friends and neighbours out of quarantine to join them at Lottery Tickets and Whist. In fact, so eager is the youngest Miss Bennet to be out and social, it is purported that she has attempted to organise a masked ball. Howsoever, I gather there have been few sponsors.

There is one other, of my knowledge, whose conduct is pronounced equally inappropriate[*]. A recent - and favourite - acquaintance of yours, who has - it seems - been stockpiling flour and buying up salted meat, then selling these on at vast profit. As this information comes from the source aforementioned[**], not *wholly* to be relied upon, I must withhold my judgement *(somewhat)*; though it seems well within the character revealed to me over lengthy acquaintance, with no recent amendment to which I might cling.

Our loyalty is of great value, I agree. But we must take the foremost care where we bestow it. Also, our hearts.

Lady Catherine spent much of yesterday in the organisation of a recovery celebration. It was a sight to behold. Mainly because the attending guests - all three of us - were a sight to behold. Under usual circumstances, Lady Catherine experiences a biannual 'cheeriness' which usually results in a large gathering of friends, who are welcomed with open arms, treated with warmth and generosity, and then dismissed in high dudgeon a day or so later. It is an interesting ritual, but most amusing when one knows what to expect. On this occasion, my Aunt had ordered the preparation of an extravagant meal, which I regret included the pineapple I had hoped to send to you. She had prepared guest cards for each of us, upon which she had written - in her own hand - what she considered to be our most pressing faults. After supper, we were each commanded to offer a form of improvised entertainment. Out of what must surely have been utter desperation, the Colonel opted to dance, Anne to sing, and I to recite excerpts from 'The Faerie Queen.' It did not go well.

Ah, regarding Mr Collins's foray into the world of art; you need not fear. My Aunt has many paintings completed in similar fashion. Indeed, she invites such skill. Rest-assured, he would do far worse to present her otherwise.

Regarding happiness: my grounds at Pemberley, sincere friendship *(even with one who laughs at me, knowing that I might not always bear it well)*, a sense of freedom (intangible as that may seem), my sister Georgiana, the conviction that I am of value, intellectual stimulation.

(You. In spite of your unfortunate heritage. You.)

Yours etc.

P.S. Answer: I doubt it. If you whole-heartedly believe something to be true, then life will prove it so. Thus, a belief in loss may result only in further absence.

P.P.S. I enclose an epistle from Colonel Fitzwilliam, who wishes to assure himself that you are well.

Letter Thirteen

Friday 22nd May, Hunsford Parsnip

Dear Sir,

Unfortunately, what you relate accords with what I too have heard *(thoughtless, thoughtless Lydia!)*. I am disappointed by Mr Denny. I thought he was of sounder character; and I think both my sister and he may grossly have misunderstood the purpose of masks.

I have always been able to find a place of allowing in my heart for Lydia. Foolish as she may be, I never previously considered her quite so devoid of the kindness and compassion that binds us each to other. She speaks a great deal about not caring, and now I must believe her. She brings dishonour upon my family and heaven knows what repercussions await when all this Unmentionableness is at an end. She who has broken quarantine again and again without thought or concern for others. I do not fear for my family. They are made of sterner stuff than one might think. But where so many who have so little abide resolutely by the edict, she, who has so much, does not. Perhaps you will say that she is 'but fifteen'; but I can promise you that she will be just the same when she is 'but sixty'!

But then, we all have our foibles, do we not? We are all foolish at times, or careless. But there is - ultimately - growth in it. The on-going pulse of personality. There must be growth. Otherwise, there are only ever-increasing loops *(my mind is going in loops)*.

How-ever shall I forgive her?

As a matter of fact, I *have* heard of others who do not abide by the Edict. Meryton's rather lately disgraced Master of Ceremonies is one, I hear, often to be spotted keeping assignations with his most recent mistress. But the less said of him, or his rather singular vessel, the better.

I doubt the acquaintance[*] in question has done any such thing. Or if he has, then indeed it is simply an action taken to assist others; to distribute produce fairly. If the source of which you speak is one whom I suspect[**], she will no doubt have little to say in favour of a person who acts in trade. We understand one another only as far as our prejudices allow, do we not? I will not ask you to relent in your aversion, but simply to consider if it serves you still?

I feel I have been most frivolous regarding the Unmentionable. From a distance, it is easy to imagine it a fiction. Something that all abide by out of duty, but not for any true necessity. In our isolation, within the country, it can be easy to...look away. Charlotte and Maria's Grandmama has... departed this world. She was ill only a week. Their mother is left in the greatest remorse, having been unable to attend. All are devastated. I met her many times at home. She was a dear woman - kind and generous. I am a foolish, flighty person.

Now to Mr Collins *(oh how I do hide behind Mr Collins...)*.

Mr Collins, it seems, has little knowledge of the local flora and fauna, in spite of possessing many books describing such. Thus, I found him out early this morning, waving a large axe towards a gentle row of Hawthorne and Hazelnut trees near the border of the Hunsford grounds. Upon rushing towards him and voicing seven-foot-distant protests, I discovered he considered his near-victims not trees, but 'weeds.' I undeceived him immediately. 'Are the trees in the field human, that they should be besieged by you?' I cried. Truly, I have been too much alone. He was most taken aback, responding that he had no intention of besieging anyone, least of all 'you, dear cousin Elizabeth. For family, and the accord within, is everything.' Which would have been plenty, indeed pleasantry, enough had he not felt obliged to add that 'within family, one must prepare oneself for all forms of irrationality, and unreasonability, and irascibility, especially among the women-folk; and tolerance and forgiveness one must practice and have readily to hand, to soothe those fevered, feeble brows commanded to one's charge.' With this he dropt the axe and made his way in haste towards the house, where he no doubt went at once to Charlotte with complaint. Once I had hidden the axe away forever and for good, I reflected upon our system of education, that teaches the young so little of the plants and trees and creatures within our trust. Mr Collins might - and does - furnish one with the quasi-accurate date of any battle, whether requested or no. But is this truly a useful, transferable intelligence, I wonder, comparatively speaking?

I have yet two letters from Kitty, another from my father and a small package from Jane to read and respond to. Thus, we are told that the post will soon cease for the time being, so our knowledge of friends and family becomes utterly restricted. Please know that my daily thoughts and prayers include your sister.

I am very glad of this correspondence. Thank you.

Yours etc.

P.S. Please do not reproach yourself for the pineapple. I am sure we would not have had the first idea how to eat it. I only wish I might have been present at your Aunt's gathering. Howsoever, seeing it in my mind's eye must be pleasure enough.

P.P.S. I am pleased to receive Colonel Fitzwilliam's letter and enclose my reply.

Letter Fourteen

Saturday 23rd May, Rosings Confessional

Dear Madam,

Firstly, please convey my deepest condolences to Mrs Collins, Miss Lucas and, when you may, all at Lucas Lodge.

Second, please accept my unreserved apology for any ill-judged remarks regarding said acquaintance. I am sure you are right, and you do well to remind me that anyone may make a truth out of anything - with due repetition.

If I may venture; you sound somewhat distressed. This circumstance is trying for each and all of us, and you have borne through with infinite patience and humour. Do not give up.

You have my deepest appreciation regarding Georgiana. My last communication - for the present - was, as your elder sister's, all calmness and reassurance.

My answer to your new understanding of the unfolding of the Unmentionable is 'how could you know prior?' Or any of us. For my part, I would always rather hear of a resolute attention to the good or amusing, fanciful as it may seem, than dire portents aiding misery to spread. We must be kinder. Universally kinder. We all have differing experiences and, therefore, differing levels of understanding. Some will go through the entirety of lockdown without knowing what is now revealed to you. Others will come yet closer; know more. Of my acquaintance, few have contracted the actual illness. But I have heard of many who have succumbed to despair and the unnatural pain of isolation. For this, we are informed, the government is to blame. But how could they do better without the hindsight all have lacked? We must be kinder. Have more faith. It is always easy to imagine a better course, post incarnation.

This from my father, years ago, may bring you comfort; 'we cannot allow ourselves to view ourselves through any eyes other than our own, and those eyes must be ever loving and kind.'

In terms of forgiveness, I have an answer which may, perhaps, surprise you. We forgive others for our own sake first. I had a grandfather who was dear to me. Both dear to me, and not. And I to he. We fought through similarity and difference. For months we did not speak at all. But when he died, I felt only filiality - was left with only love. The disappointment I had felt at times, the disparity, the frustration, all evaporated in an instant and I knew only fondness. This left me many months experience of the most profound regret, which haunts me yet. Had I been master of myself. Had I esteemed more, and quarrelled less, been guilty of less vanity and pride, I might look back with greater peace. Had I forgiven him fully, completely, when I might; cherishing his humanity beyond all else.

(Your letters are the most precious moments of my day... I think of you... constantly... regarding what I might say... in correspondence. I...)

I thank you too.

Yours etc.

P.S. Enclosed is a further communication from the Colonel. I trust the news from home and town was all that you might hope?

P.P.S. I enclose what are left of Mrs Norris's Banbury cakes and hope they are to your taste. Lady Catherine has insisted on Anne's being placed upon a strict purge to counter any ill-effects occurring during her absence. Thus, we are to eat only Pease-soup, gruel and boiled turnips for the foreseeable future.

P.P.P.S. The Master of Ceremonies - a rascal? One would not think it to look at him. Of what vessel do you speak?

Letter Fifteen

Monday 25th May, Hunsford Place of Purgatory

Dear Sir,

I thank you for your apology, however unnecessary. The fault is mine for putting pen to paper in such a humour. I hope you will burn the letter, if you have not already done so.

I was saddened to hear of your Grandpapa, and of your remorse since. If it is of any comfort, I sincerely do not believe that resentments, large or small, live beyond our time here. Only love.

Yes, I thank you - satisfactory news from both home and town. Kitty has discovered a taste for baking and thus, she informs me, has had to let out each of her gowns. Jane sent a beautifully embroidered mask for each of us at Hunsford, carefully stitched by her own dear hand. She mentioned having received, at last, a brief letter from Miss Bingley *(in response to a far longer one from her)*. Jane continues brave and steady and, I am certain, as slender as she ever was.

Incidentally, the Banbury Cakes were delicious. Thank you for sending them. You must all have experienced great disappointment at their removal. I enclose, in return, some cheese cakes - made by Charlotte and I this afternoon. As they are a gift, they may not be sent back or redistributed. Guard them well.

My father writes that his unrelieved solitude palls and he is considering the commencement of a tunnel from his library to town. The thought exhausts him - especially having only access to cutlery as tools. I have responded that just because the completion of a matter may take 'a month of Sundays,' does not mean it should not be commenced. But as my father hates town, I do wonder if his motivation for said tunnel is misplaced. I confess myself compelled to encourage him, as he may reach town in time to stop Lydia from accomplishing something particularly foolish. But I grow delusional, on both counts.

On the subject of my father, I am sure he would both agree with your thoughts on government culpability and disagree. Both most fervently. He has never had any faith at all in any governing body, believing that the very people most attracted to, or inheriting, such a path in life are the very last people who should ever be in possession of such power. He equally believes that the lack of foresight inherent in many - and the study of history leading, somehow, to the making of much the same errors again - indicates that no person should ever be in charge of another, let alone an entire governing body. When asked what we might have instead, by way of social structure, he invariably replies 'why, I've no idea, my Lizzy. But, thankfully, that is not for me to determine,' - and returns once more to his library. Really, I think he is mostly speaking of Mama.

I was moved by your words upon forgiveness. How often we may wish to forgive, but do not out of fear and pride. How often may we wish, privately, to be better than we are - only then to publicly fall short.

Grief is strange. Charlotte and Maria are intermittently beside themselves, then as if nothing has happened. Of a sudden I may come across one or other standing stock still in the midst of the garden, staring at the ground. There were letters of condolence, but not so many as one might expect - some offered comfort, others not quite so. All meant well, I believe. I do understand - what can one possibly say? But always better to say something of... affection, however brief. One, from a cousin declared 'I know not what to say. Thus, I send only love.' It is the one letter Charlotte has kept. Charlotte has asked me to stop smiling at her. 'Eliza,' she has said on several occasions 'there's that sad, half smile that is new between us. Put it away.' I wish I might embrace her... But at present, that is Mr Collins' privilege alone. Here it must be chronicled, that while he may not always say what might be best, his actions - under this circumstance - are truly quite attentive, for he is often to be seen tottering nearby, ready to give his lady an affectionate - if awkward - pat.

How much I now look forward to. Such simple, vital things. The freedom to offer comfort to those I love. The freedom to express affection. The desire to vary my attire - not just on wash day. The freedom to go to Meryton; to see the dear, familiar faces. We are so attached to this life. There is much I can see in my mind's eye, of the world beyond Hunsford, but it will not do; I must have reality again.

Yours etc.

P.S. A rascal indeed. He has a small dwelling, by the Lea, at the farthest end of his estate, and has frequently been spotted casting off in a small punt from t'other side of said dwelling, whereupon he crouch-paddles his way to his mistress's house. As the river flows past Aunt Phillips's home, the whole village are aware. I confess, I was surprised as you. At local gatherings, he seemed all affability and devotion to his family. But Aunt Philips - ever alert - caught him passing 'notes' to Mary King at an assembly late last year and all was revealed - countless mistresses, of which his wife was all too aware. It transpired that, when first discovered, he had called her 'mad as old King George' and threatened not only to inform the whole of Meryton of her 'insanity,' but also to have her locked away 'for the good of the children.' Hence her dedicated silence. The man is clearly a follower of Fordyce. We all still hope he will find his way out to sea. *(Gracious, I sound like Mama...)*

P.P.S. The swifts have arrived. I look forward to them every year, and this year they are more welcome than ever - their calls of joy announcing the summer.

P.P.P.S. My reply to the Colonel is enclosed.

Letter Sixteen

Tuesday 26th May, Rosings Sanctuary of Muffled Mutterings

Dear Madam,

I am most grateful for your letter and generous words *(I could never burn a letter of yours, but that is a secret between these walls and I)*. I am in complete agreement. I remind myself constantly of the same. There are no grudges yonder and regret, beyond reflection and resolution, serves no useful purpose and, therefore, must be set aside.

Regarding your father; a tunnel sounds a useful, if lengthy, proposition. We have two known tunnels at Pemberley. One from the kitchens to the stables. Another from the library to what was once the Housekeeper's cottage - such an obvious place for a secret door and passageway that it remained undisclosed for two generations. We have yet to learn its purpose, though all have the same suspicion.

Speaking of which, the Master of Punting would be, it seems, a man who perhaps should never have married. My father adored my Mother, and she he. I was blessed to have that example. My Uncle was less fortunately situated. He too exhibited a tendency to question the sanity of his wives, whilst taxing that sanity to the very limit. My father once said that he felt his brother - and all around him - might have lived far better and with greater peace had he not, originally, felt such obligation to be married. We are all so varied in our inclinations that a rigorous social structure to which all must adhere seems, often, to cause more pain than good. Thus, we return once more to kindness and allowance. If my Uncle had felt more harmony within, and was, thus, able to express himself freely and with truth, his ripples in the world would have been likewise of peace and truth instead. So too with Fordyce.

I am thankful to learn that all remains well with your family in both Meryton and town. Miss Bingley, as a favour to me, was employed in writing daily - and lengthy - greetings to my sister - now made impossible with the cessation of the post. This, perhaps, explains, somewhat, the brevity of her correspondence with Miss Bennet.

Anne, too, has been engaged in mask making. Hers, however, are for her own distinct use and seem, predominantly, to be a device deployed to infuriate her mother, who is now unable to discern a word she says. This gives my cousin the free reign you wished for her, to speak whatsoever she desires without fear of repercussion. Until recently, I had firmly believed that Anne's frustrations resided within her own conviction of having a weak constitution from birth, but it has since transpired that she feels - most fervently - that this is a notion wholly enforced upon her. My family, on my Father's side, are blessed with the most acute hearing, and I am thus - unfortunately - able to hear what Lady Catherine cannot. I say 'unfortunately,' because Anne has rather a ready wit and I dare not laugh before my Aunt or I will give my cousin away.

I am delighted to hear that Mr Collins rises in your esteem, somewhat. When my father passed, I felt profound grief, but also isolation. You are right - those of close acquaintance know not what best to say, so they depart, swiftly, and rather completely. At a time when liveliness might most be welcome, it is withdrawn - for fear too, I believe - a superstition that loss might be contagious, unsubstantiated as that may be. We do not need words from others at such times, for words will never do. But to be *present*, ready to offer affection, even humour, why *that* is of the truest, highest value.

I might add, yet, that through such isolation, my sister and I grew deeply close. Thus, there is always light.

Yours etc.

P.S. I enclose further greetings from the Colonel.

P.P.S. The Rosings inmates were all most deeply grateful for the cheese cakes, which were exceptional. Thank you.

Letter Seventeen

Friday 29th May, Hunsford Villa of Liberty Givers (& Takers)

Dear Sir,

Precisely! As a general rule, I do my best to not concern myself with that I cannot help. I have seldom found it to change anything for the better, but have likewise noticed that the successful deflection of my mind provides, at the very least, a strong sense of relief instead. When we sincerely love, we wish the very best for the objects of our affection - but, in the muddle of life, our petty concerns can confuse and misdirect our feelings. With the release of these concerns, love remains. But I repeat myself. You speak of allowance and kindness. As your Papa once said, you must give this to yourself and think only of the past as its remembrance gives you pleasure. Truly.

I would offer a suggestion, regarding Miss de Bourgh and her application of masks, which you are at liberty to take or leave. Your cousin seeks expression for her frustrations, but may not do so directly for fear of repercussion. I am certain that she will never find lasting peace or happiness while she believes your Aunt's approval to be the source of either. I fear she is unlikely ever to have Lady Catherine's compassion towards her will for, if readily available, it would have shown itself by now. Your cousin's self-compassion, however, is inherently assured, if she will allow it. When she is able to release her anger, privately, and to turn away from the past - which cannot be helped - towards the future - which can – then, I believe, she will find a place of lasting self-assurance; and should she find her mother still intractable, it will not matter so.

I appreciate your words on the Master of Paddles. A new perspective is always refreshing. Although I cannot offer sympathy with his behaviour, I may with the root of it. The questioning of the sanity of his wife as an aid to concealment, however, is a matter beyond my acceptance. On this, Mama and I are *(for once!)* in complete agreement. She was particularly shocked, indeed, to learn that such matters were discussed before his children. 'Does he not consider, Mr Bennet,' she has exclaimed to Papa on *several* occasions, 'that the children might *believe it* and then consider it their own *inescapable* future? I would not do a child of mine so *great* a *wrong* for *all the world*.' She can be quite wise, Mama, on the subject of children.

I have had cause, recently, as you may know, to consider a path that did not feel my own, for the sake of others[***]. For the briefest moment, I felt the weight many feel almost constantly, to make a decision that does not accord with their idea of happiness, and desires for their own future. There is a stubbornness about me, however, which I cherish - for I will not be intimidated by the will of another. I allowed myself freedom, sanctioned by Papa. I am forever grateful to him. I know for certain now, what instinct alone guided me towards before. That had I bent to the will of another, looked to another for my own path in this life, my unhappiness would have been great indeed. We must allow ourselves choice. We must understand also, that where there is uncertainty, there is often no decision yet to make.

Now that Mr Collins has recovered fully from the Unmentionable, he has begun an intense investigation as to its originator. Mama behaves similar whenever she contracts a cold. The household is thoroughly interrogated, staff included, until she determines the culprit - usually Kitty - and holds them to account by grumbling. His current favourites are a household from Rochester, who moved 'lock, stock and barrel' last week 'in a cart with rusty wheels drawn by an *old nag*, Charlotte - and before the hallowed walls of

Rosings,' has been his constant lament (we hear his sobs at night). The fact that they should not have moved during lockdown has not escaped his notice. The fact that they were many miles hence when he contracted the Unmentionable, has. 'Charlotte, they have a bath in the garden!' He cries in despair. 'What a pleasure that must be, dear, in the summer months,' she responds without a pause. 'Charlotte, their eldest child plays the violin very ill indeed.' 'What a pleasure that will be, dear, when he is older and more proficient.' 'Charlotte, they are all so terribly loud all of the time.' 'Why, we are all louder than we know, my dear. Go into your study and close your eyes for an hour or so.' Upon investigation of my own, it transpires that Mr Collins has a dislike of those from the north of Kent - impossible to comprehend why.

It transpires that another near neighbour may, or may not, have been feeding Mr Collins's geese. It is no wonder really, as he has shown a tendency to tether creatures, that they might conspire to flee to more exalted ground. One must never underestimate the ricochet which occurs when attempting to force to one's will a being who considers itself inherently free.

Speaking of which, Felicity is once more fully at liberty. I had it arranged that as soon as Mr Collins caught and collared her again, either myself, Charlotte or Maria - indeed, whomsoever was nearest - would instantly free her once more. After many days' amusement, Mr Collins finally relented in exhaustion and is now furious with me. He has ceased all verbal communication and avoids me, but to leave letters upon the drawing room table or under my door referring to _his_, underlined several times, cat. Charlotte assures me that Felicity was always feral and that Mr Collins paid her no heed prior except for the odd kick, but he is not to be reasoned with.

Thus, I fear, you spoke too soon regarding his rise in my esteem.

Yours etc.

P.S. My reply to the Colonel is enclosed. I expect we might see you all, at a safe distance, on Sunday for Mr Collins's eagerly-anticipated missive from the church tower?

P.P.S. It is a long held and rather foolish belief that a man in possession of a donkey must be in want of a dog. I just thought you should know.

Letter Eighteen

Saturday 30th May, Rosings Temple of Concord (which may - I trust - fare better than The Hugh Temple of Peace)

Dear Madam,

I confess, I too am curious as to how Mr Collins came by the Unmentionable. Especially as both yourself, and the Lucas sisters have, thankfully, avoided the same. So too concerning we three miscreants and her Ladyship.

Unlike Mr Collins, however, Lady Catherine has no need to conduct an intensive investigation, having decided long ago that she most likely contracted the Unmentionable from either myself or the Colonel, being interlopers to Rosings. The Colonel, particularly, has been most unpopular since her recovery, although this may be as a result of his ill-conceived celebration dance.

Yesterday, Anne - owing to that extensive morning thunderstorm - returned early from outdoor exercise to discover Mrs Norris within her chamber, overseen by my Aunt, searching through possessions hidden within a trunk. Inevitably, to my Aunt's horror and dismay, these included several questionable books, two by notorious lexicographers Messrs Head and Grose. I am sure neither publication is known to you, so I will go no further. Suffice it to say, there were heated words exchanged, unhampered by any lack of clarity or volume.

In the evening, having had no clear platform yet to offer your ideas to Anne, I took it upon myself to act as mediator between my Aunt and she. I am now in a similar position to yourself regarding Mr Collins, for neither will speak a word to me; but there is at least peace, of a kind.

(Much to my incredulity) I am in agreement with your Mama regarding the protection of young minds. Indeed, I am furnished, it seems, with an example first hand; for Anne, having evolved beside a mother who never forgets the slightest slight, is herself - at present - completely immersed in every wrong ever done to her, whether intended or no. A circumstance most surely intensified by both our continuing confinement - with no clear knowledge of when it might end - and the dampness which has replaced the early days of blue skies and warmth.

The Colonel has been called away to attend to 'a ripple of unrest,' where - he was not at liberty to say, but he has given his full assurance that there is no cause whatsoever for alarm and nothing out of the ordinary (could anything at present be described as ordinary?). Thus, he wishes you to know - regretfully - that he will not be in attendance tomorrow morn and that the letter I enclose will be his last for a time. I may not hazard a guess as to where he is sent, or for what; indeed, it would be foolish of me so to do. We must be of good cheer and hold faith with his words.

Question: If you might steer change in the world in but three ways, which would you choose?

It may *(or may not)* amuse you to hear that Miss Bingley - having uncovered a pronounced aptitude for illustration in her brother's Valet - has commissioned the man, in addition to his present duties, to sketch her in a series of 'lockdown ensembles,' and then reproduce these to send to a multitude of correspondents. I have little idea why I am one such recipient, having not the slightest interest in fashion. Perhaps I might send them on to you?

Yours etc.

P.S. I thank you, regarding the dog and donkey. I am now much the wiser.

P.P.S. I fear my Aunt and Mr Collins are likely to have an agreement of the most violent kind regarding your recent neighbours. Mrs Norris first drew our attention to their freshly renovated dwelling at breakfast, informing her ladyship that in her (humble) opinion it was 'an abomination of the very worst kind.' My Aunt was out of the house and within her carriage before one might say 'multum stercora in parvum spatium.'

She returned pale and speechless.

Letter Nineteen

Monday 1st June, Hunsford Cove of Conciliatory Gestures

Dear Sir,

I thank you for your letter and, indeed, that of the Colonel, which contained many more reassurances. At this stage in lockdown, it is not difficult to imagine what might be the cause of 'unrest.' We are very fortunate here. You are right, we must - as ever - keep in the best of spirits and trust.

I am unsure quite how to respond to your news regarding your Aunt and Miss de Bourgh. Perhaps silence between the two is best, for the present. At times, there are simply no worthy words left to one.

Mama has a distant relation who does much the same in correspondence as Miss Bingley. Whenever a letter is received, it invariably contains a recent sketch of the lady, drawn by her sister. As accomplished as they are, Mama is ever baffled as to what to do with them – 'I simply do not understand, my dear Mr Bennet,' she will invariably say 'why she should think I need so many. I shall not thank her next time, and perhaps she will grasp the hint.' Adding 'I do so dislike people who force me to be rude.' At last count, she had three-hundred and fifty-one, and is yet afraid to dispose of them for fear the lady may, of a sudden, visit. Thus, to your kind offer and having, possibly, even less interest in fashion than you - I answer; no, thank you.

I must agree, I infinitely preferred quarantine in the sunshine with the bright blue sky. As refreshing as it is to listen to the wind howling round the house at night, rather than Mr Collins, I would welcome another long spell of clear skies and gentle warmth.

Actually, I *am* familiar with both Head and Grose. When I was but ten years old Papa loaned me - ever curious - a copy of Grose's 'Dictionary of the Vulgar Tongue' from his library. I spent many hours exploring its substance and thus, thanks to Papa and Mr Grose, I know expressions to this day that might shame a sailor. So, you see - impressionable. Mama was utterly horrified when she found out. For a year, she would not take me into town for fear I might forget myself. Papa also loaned me an extremely old book from his collection by Robert Greene entitled 'The Black Bookes Messenger,' concerning the exploits of one Ned Browne. I remember little of it now, although it was duly scandalous, excepting the opening expression 'read and be warned, laugh as you like, judge as you find,' which I adored and adopted.

Coincidentally, Mr Collins has engaged Charlotte's assistance in compiling a new dictionary of 'proper expressions,' fancying himself something of a lexicographer. While Charlotte is happy to have him engaged in so engrossing a project, she does cherish hopes that it may - in time and with the right encouragement - make for a more solitary pursuit.

In spite of previous weather bewails, it was well indeed that Sunday's sermon was so relentlessly, loudly wet, for it ensured that those who remained before their own houses and at a substantial distance from Mr Collins and the 'Lady Catherine Trumpet' (namely, all but we three women and, possibly the Rosings carriage) were unable to hear his extensive missive regarding 'interlopers' and 'unwelcome guests.' Hardly biblical of him. I trust that your Aunt and cousin were comfortable within and found the rather sodden Lady Catherine acoustically effective. Had it not been for the weather, his invention might have been something of a triumph. For our part, we did our best to divert our minds from the moment he cried out 'for aliens have entered, the holy places of the Lord's house!'

and pointed directly at the innocents from Rochester...

'Would you excuse me while I go and scream into a pillow?' murmured Charlotte, once we returned home.

This is now a common phrase of hers. It began, most particularly, when she endeavoured to encourage Mr Collins in the washing of his hands often and throughout the day. Although Mr Collins adheres to certain rudimentary cleansing rituals, he does not by any means consider the washing of hands as a necessity. Charlotte has an inkling that it is mostly through unwashed hands that infection is actually spread, but finds her husband resolutely unwilling even to consider such a suggestion. 'Why my dearest and then more dear than dear,' he says, winningly, 'you know as well as any that sickness is conveyed through miasma,' and with that he takes her hand, looks deeply into her eyes and speaks very slowly and gently. 'Let me most *patiently* and *infinitely* assure you that - when un-gloved - my hands are always rigorously perfumed with Truefitt & Hill's Freshman Cologne' (a gift from your Aunt, it would seem). Charlotte's most recent attempt to convince him was met with an upsurge of frustration 'do you think me a Pontius?' he exclaimed, quickly adding 'my dear.'

Charlotte, Maria and I have passed the greater part of this afternoon in conciliatory baking for those from Rochester, which we will leave upon their doorstep. I cannot imagine it is enough to compensate for such unnecessary unkindness. Mr Collins himself is not to be reasoned with, and although, as aforementioned, it is highly likely that they did not hear, they must surely have seen his gesture.

Answer: I have no great wish to change the world, only myself, as I may. That being said, it has been most amusing to consider, so these are my thoughts - first, dancing allowed for married couples to encourage continuing affection and vitality; second, no more entailments, or, indeed, Wills of any kind, only goodwill; third, infinite opportunity for all, no matter whom or where, teaching all to fish, metaphorically speaking... Oh, and no more disease, of course, compulsory handwashing, the rigorous vetting of clergymen for a reasonable level of personal appeal, all repetitive rascals to grow a moustache, that they might instantly be recognisable and deflected - may I really only have three?

It is Maria's birthday tomorrow, and we plan to surprise her with a small celebration. She has been rather anxious of late, understandably, and we hope to compensate in some small way for the absence of her full family.

Yours etc.

P.S. I enclose my reply to the Colonel's letter and ask that you leave it wheresoever he may swiftly discover it upon his return****.

P.P.S. As a matter of very idle curiosity, where did you find yourself upon Sunday morning, that you were unable to attend Mr Collins's soaking?

Letter Twenty

Tuesday 2nd June, Rosings Residence of Righteousness

Dear Madam,

I thank you for your letter and wish to assure you, first and foremost, of my presence on Sunday morn. Stationed beneath a far oak tree, I bore witness to the whole. You speak the truth, had it not been for the weather, I am convinced the Lady Catherine would have carried Mr Collins's voice to the very farthest reaches of the parish. Thus, we were blessed. Lady Catherine herself - who, unlike myself, was able to hear the sermon in its entirety - was quite delighted by it; both - I am given to understand from her jubilant retelling - the extensive portion referring to her astonishing resurrection, and that concerning your neighbours. It seems your cousin outdid himself, on both counts. Please accept my earnest pledge to add to your conciliatory gifts at the earliest opportunity. *(utterly inexcusable!)*

I would imagine there is right in Mrs Collins's theorising - she seems a regular James Lind - one of the few admirable Physicians of my knowledge. Perhaps Mr Collins might concede that miasma and transferral from hands are *each* likely causes? I must confess, it perplexes one in the extreme to imagine a person scrupulous in daily washing, who does not then - also - regularly cleanse their hands. It seems as much an oddity to me as a gentleman who endures all the rigours of formal dress, only to leave his home barefoot.

My father was an honourable man; broad-minded, and generous. When I was little more than four, I remember his escorting me on a tour of our estate, to show what one day would be within my care. He spoke at length of our immense responsibility to others, and what that must signify; 'to be placed at the head of... aught - a household, an estate, a country, even, one must always recognize the great gift of trust given, and repay that trust with kindness, with constancy and integrity,' he said. I have never forgotten it, and have done everything I can *(I hope)* to live by his words. You are quite correct, unrest has always the self-same basis.

When my mother passed, my father became suddenly less sure of himself. At times, he was susceptible to rather evident falsehoods. Not, I hasten to add, to the detriment of any within his care, but more to his own. Of that I will no further speak. I will tell you, instead, of his passing. I have never spoken of this to anyone. Not even

Georgiana, who was too young at the time, and then I never had the heart... When my father grew ill, I was advised to engage an acclaimed physician (for, as I now know, much credence for intelligence is given to those who speak freely of the ominous or grim - examine, if you will, our Scandal Sheets). The prognosis he gave was bleak. He had seen the case before, on several occasions, and was able to tell me, and, most unfortunately, my father - how it would all fall out for him. This he did in immense detail and without my permission - for I was away one day on business that could not wait *(but one day!)*. When I discovered his action, I was enraged - more so than I ever have been, before or since. But the damage was done. This man was employed to tend to my father, to give him care - not to frighten and to leave him without hope. There can be no *care* in that! That he proclaimed would happen did so swiftly and with absolute accuracy. My father moved from moderate symptoms to the worst of cases, within a matter of days. I hope never to feel so *powerless* again. Had I hired a physician of lesser reputation, but greater humility, greater compassion, I am convinced my father could have lived.

You are right - utterly. You cannot trust another to make a decision for your future. You must seek clarity within, that you may not be so easily affected by their *tutored* paradigms.

———

Yes, only three allowed. Those are the rules! Dancing for married couples would not have occurred to me, but I must agree - indeed, it is the only dancing that truly appeals to me. A world without Wills might be somewhat chaotic. But Wills of goodwill only, I concede, would be preferable. How does one determine, however, what goodwill is exactly? What might be goodwill for one could easily appear not so to another. Agreed, regarding a universal teaching to fish; self-sufficiency is vital. Now, at the risk of appearing unchivalrous, if all rascals are to grow a moustache, how then are we to know a female rascal? A beauty patch might be an obvious suggestion, but I hear they are so easily removed or lost.

I too would eliminate disease, also unpaid labour - when all must eat, house and clothe themselves, it seems insupportable to expect a person to work for nought. Then I might lessen the penalties for petty theft, which are quite ludicrously harsh (especially among those who have little as it is), and introduce penalties, instead, for those who are careless with the hearts of others. But perhaps that is rather draconian of me.

I am most deeply, profoundly shocked by your early reading. One could not think it possible to look at you. I have never heard of Mr Greene's publication, but am tempted to seek it out that I might come to know more fully to what horrors you have been exposed. Your Papa is surely a most liberal guardian.

Yours etc.

P.S. I do hope your birthday celebration for Maria was as pleasant as possible. Is it usual to you to celebrate such an event? In our household, we might mark the anniversary with a small remembrance, but only Lady Catherine (depending upon mood) will have a gathering.

Letter Twenty-one

Thursday 4th June, Hunsford Parlour of Impertinence

Dear Sir,

I am greatly relieved to hear that you were, indeed, present on Sunday. It seemed most afflicting to imagine that you might have had the good sense to spare yourself, whilst the rest of us did not. I am sure your conciliatory contribution will be greatly appreciated by our neighbours. Of whom more, presently.

The gardens seem to have exploded over this recent week, passing from relative order to abundant chaos. In frustration on Tuesday noon, Mr Collins turned the goats loose to combat the overgrowth, with - naturally - mixed results (that could be his epitaph). Goats, it transpires, are imprecise as to where they choose to mow and seem all too taken with whatever Mr Collins treasures most. Thus, I inadvertently won my way back - briefly - into his good books, by glancing early from my window and spying Evan and Tilly both headed with unprecedented purpose towards his prized artichokes. Having raised the alarm, the household - in unity - ran outside and pulled both extremely strong and stubborn nannies away and guided them towards greener pastures. Mr Collins was quite beside himself with gratitude at the preservation of 'so *modern* a vegetable, cousin Elizabeth.' Once he had finished weeping, he noticed - to his intense mortification - that Maria was still in her dressing-gown. He passed the afternoon locked within his study composing a sermon on the incontrovertible slide towards impropriety in unmarried women. I know this, because there was a new note upon the drawing room table expressing such.

This morning the goats had at the artichokes again, this time with pronounced success. A distraught Mr Collins stumbled the garden, wringing his hands, attempting to establish just how they had escaped their enclosure. It is true, a goat can climb rather well, but as a general rule these ones are rather docile, contented beings and seldom bother. After an hour or more, he discovered, at last, the frayed rope to their gateway hung like bunting across the archway to our Rochester-neighbours' grounds. They had even draped wild roses delicately athwart. 'So, it begins,' gasped Mr Collins, having started it.

This afternoon was passed by the Parson of Hunsford, in the assembly of a grand sign on which was painted large 'TRESPASSERS WILL NOT BE TOLERATED.' He might as well have written 'Neighbours.' It was barely dry and hung where his adversaries might best see it, before an effigy of Mr Collins, stuffed with straw, was brought out and deposited in the aforementioned bathtub with a sign across his chest indicating 'BLOCKHEAD.' They had even fashioned him a small papier-mâché trumpet. The real Mr Collins was speechless.

'If only I could believe this might be an end to it,' murmured Charlotte to the sky.

My Papa is a liberal man, in many ways, you are quite correct. This he attributes to his mother, my grandmama, who was of so open a mind, so free a-tendency of speech, that Mama could hardly bear to have her in the house. 'People are changeable, dear Lizzy,' she would say to me, 'people are changeable. They mean well, most all of them. But do not pin your hopes on any one of them. Trust to yourself and all will fall out well. Trust to another (nodding at Mama), and you will find yourself at the mercy of their current whim.'

My father's present reinterpretation of her words seems thoroughly apt in terms of Mr Collins; 'human-beings, my Lizzy, have a tendency to censure one another in excess, only to weep with outrage and shout for vengeance when their turn comes,' adding, in case I had forgot, 'I want nothing to do with most of them.'

Mr Collins has spent the last three hours scything down any branches within our neighbours' grounds that have had the temerity to invade either our property or the green (you may remember that I have hidden his axe). He really is the most foolish man. It is now after ten and he is still without, though it is almost dark. He will be fortunate to return with all his limbs.

Maria has contracted a slight indisposition, we believe after Sunday's soaking, or perhaps owing to the dressing-gown extravaganza and ensuing humiliation. Thus, she spent most of her birthday within her chamber, wrapped in a quilt. When her condition worsened overnight, Charlotte administered warm wine throughout the next day, a Lucas family medication made from last year's elderberries. This proved quite the restorative. Charlotte and I are now rather more enlightened than we ever wished to be as to the contents of Maria's correspondence with my youngest sister, which she half-sang to us, and seems - at least in part - responsible for her recent anxiety. I thank heaven, after all, that the post was stopped. Lydia is most ingenious in covering a sheet of paper in minutely written tattle. If only women might seek employment (factories aside!), she would be assured of an infinite income among the Scandal Sheets of your mentioning.

With regard to your father, I am truly sorry. Yet you must not blame yourself. We are each of us encouraged to believe that those in positions of trust or authority are able to comprehend fully what course is best for others. You could not have known. With the temporary exception of Lydia, who does not seem to learn, I wish all might be easier within themselves for that which could not have been foreseen - and with one another. Shame and blame do make the most dreadful circle. Besides, at this time and distance, having no longer a clear and thorough memory of your exact feelings, the extreme level of duress you were most clearly under, who are you to act as judge upon yourself, to relitigate your case?

Regarding goodwill, I am inclined to think it not a subject for debate. I concede that certain beings might be unimpressed by 'sentimentalities' that they consider weakness, but that is up to them. Kindness is kindness, and needs no credential.

Over the identifier of a female rascal, I admit to being torn. Being, likely, so grossly outnumbered by her male counterparts, I feel she might be allowed to wander at liberty until the ratio is equalized. If not, then perhaps some foliage - evergreen. A pin made of laurel leaves, or spruce? A beauty patch is rather old fashioned and might send the wrong signal, don't you think?

I confess, you seem of a more liberal turn than I imagined (although perhaps not regarding dancing). In an attempt to commence the elimination of unpaid labour, I have mentioned to Mr Collins that he might consider a wage for Charlotte - not as his wife, of course (for that is of her own election), but as his... everything else. Should he ever make acknowledgement of my enquiry, I shall let you know.

I wonder when you might hear again from the Colonel?

Yours etc.

P.S. Respectfully, please do not refer to Mr Collins as my 'cousin' in future correspondence. If I myself have done so, then I apologise. It has been quite unconscious and unintentionally done.

P.P.S. Do you find your frustrations exaggerate in lockdown? I fear I become more and more like my cousin.

P.P.P.S. Oh bother.

Letter Twenty-two

Friday 5th June, Rosings Stockade

Dear Madam,

I trust that Miss Lucas is soon recovered. At least it is not the Unmentionable.

It seems that lockdown has now worn thin for my Aunt and she has decided that it simply must come to an end. The government cannot dare to argue, and will surely follow suit. She has - somehow - persuaded her Steward to leave his family and return to his duties, thus the last two days have been filled with the urgent - and unnecessary - rearrangement of furniture and, indeed, of all of us. It has been most bewildering. The Colonel is, perhaps, fortunate to have been called away. My Aunt has determined that the grounds will be next in her 'Maintain and Develop' programme, which might as well be called 'Wreck and Rebuild.'

I might mention that, regarding Anne, the most recent developments in the reassertion of my Aunt's authority have been rather unfortunate. After several days of quite fearsome silence between the two, Lady Catherine held her breath for an extraordinary (and slightly alarming) interval, then withdrew to her room and seated herself by a window, staring into the gloaming and refusing any attempts to restore her spirits, even by the favoured Mrs Norris. Although no actual edict of silence was issued, a dreadful hush fell upon the house and each felt compelled to move about on tiptoe. Anne was left rebellious, confused, vexed, then - of a sudden, it seemed - as though marooned. Sunken and filled with repentance, within an hour she was before her mother, almost upon her knees, promising a return to obedience and pleading for forgiveness. To this my Aunt spoke not a word, would not so much as look upon her daughter, allowing Anne a sleepless night to consider further, before sweeping downstairs the next morning with a written list of personal improvements for her daughter, to which agreement I was called upon both to proclaim and witness. Not as signatory, I hasten to add - for I could not have done so.

In order to restore my Aunt's good opinion, Anne must now devote two hours each day to embroidery. She *is* to learn the pianoforte, but in theory only - no instrument is to be played. This for an hour each day. Also, drawing - using myself as subject - every evening. Outdoor exercise is confined once more to a circuit of the local area by carriage, or she may walk sedately about the grounds for an half hour daily, but only if accompanied by myself. She may read only from a selection of specifically chosen books. Only after a week of 'significant improvement' will my Aunt agree to commence actually speaking to her daughter once more. In the meantime, I am asked to act as intermediary. Also, we are allowed no more seasoning at meal-times.

To this I might say much, but it is not my home, and I must leave well alone. My Aunt has never been one to be easily reasoned with. Having witnessed first-hand the spirit that lies dormant within Anne, I have every reason to hope that my cousin will return in full force, once the time is right.

I would add that it has become apparent that the perennial coryza to which my cousin is prone, that has haunted her all her life and given rise to a suspicion of continuing ill-health, is actually caused by nerves exacerbated by her mother. For while she is at present, for most of the waking day, to be heard sneezing almost without pause, when she had determined to rise and demonstrate that unprecedented independence of spirit, I observed not so much as a sniffle.

I *have* enjoyed a dance, upon occasion. My previous objections, however, refer to an outrageous expectation of my participation, regardless of whether I would will it or no. Concerning surprise at my liberality, I would recall your attention to a request I once made not to early sketch my character. Indeed, I hope this correspondence may provide you with greater insight, greater clarity, than previously was possible.

You have my agreement regarding a beauty spot. Indeed, their previous and enduring popularity is a subject of bewilderment to me. Thus, yes to a laurel pin. Shall I suggest this to Miss Bingley, that she might endorse and circulate the notion? So too with the moustache. We must be fair!

Forgive me, but I find myself compelled to ask; is there truth in your Meryton Aunt having started a 'Tattle Paper' to provide the local area with 'news' whilst they may not hear directly from the lady herself?

Although I have, as you surmised, blamed myself for what happened to my father, it is the frustration over my lack of knowledge and experience, and the blind trust I had in the recommendation of another, that still holds sway over my remembrance. In the attempt of this man to assume a knowledge and authority that was expected of him, but which he did not truly possess, he neglected to consider that he was first and foremost called there as protector. So too those in power and authority who oft forget their place as guardians. No, on reflection, this is not yet quite true. My greatest frustration is that I knew better, somehow, but did not attend.

That aside, I offer apology for sharing so very intimate a detail. It was inappropriate.

I am most interested to learn of your belief that a wife must have a wage. I confess to having never considered such a role as unpaid labour and thus in need of monetary exchange, although I do note your qualification.

Although it may seem that my Aunt has many and great demands upon her time, I am given to understand that she is engaged in frequent written communications with your Mr Collins. Her ideas for improvement extend, it seems, beyond Rosings and out into the parish. Indeed, I believe my Aunt to have penned the majority of tomorrow's sermon. To which, I presume, Mr Collins will add his own - aforementioned - views upon correct attire for young ladies - and effigies.

(I can put it off no longer)

I have this day received a messenger, sent by the Colonel, who is - he now confesses - installed with his regiment in Woolwich. He gives news of a small organised rally due, requesting the easing of lockdown, which he is charged to oversee. He was at great pains to assure me that every indication shows the intent to be peaceful and orderly. You see how little I am concerned, that I leave this information to the very last.

Yours etc.

P.S. As it seemed pressing, I took the opportunity to forward your recent letter to the Colonel, with my reply to his message. No doubt he will respond, when he may.

P.P.S. I agree with your Grandmama *and* your Father.

Letter Twenty-three

Saturday 6th June, Hunsford Den of Ignominy

Dear Sir,

Thank you for forwarding my letter to the Colonel. You are quite correct, there was a matter of personal import raised by the gentleman to which I require, if at all possible, a speedy answer[****].

I am not excessively surprised to hear that the unrest of which the Colonel spoke lies within London. While we await the lifting of lockdown from our positions of privilege, others will find the need of generating income, of feeding their families, infinitely more pressing. I am most thankful the intent is peaceful and hope all goes well for them. Come what may, we must all have answers soon. I confess, I too long for reassurance of my family's well-being, and am certain you must be equally impatient for news.

If I seemed to lack compassion, concerning your Papa, then it is most certainly for I to offer apology, and not for you. My frankness was inappropriate, and may perhaps be attributed to the informality achieved by a frequent written correspondence. It is easy to forget oneself, when not face to face; but that is no excuse. If I may, I simply wished to express - albeit it poorly - that whilst we might in the early days of what we consider a mistake, take some stock and resolution, to torture ourselves in later years, however, with that we cannot change, seems a misguided and painful application of our energies. Your intentions were clearly for the very best, now you must allow yourself peace. You are not my cousin - you do not offer kicks and demand love. So please, be easier with yourself *(that you might too be easier with others)*.

May I tell you of my Grandmama, as an exchange of confidence - to perhaps restore your faith in me? Like you, I have never mentioned this happening to anyone but Papa. It has always felt too private, and - perhaps - more than most might wish to know. I was present at her passing. My Papa was nearby, but had retired to his room after two day's vigil. I had been holding her hand for some time, talking over precious memories and giving thanks for the many gifts with which she had blessed me. At first, her hand would squeeze mine gently in acknowledgement, but the pulses grew gradually fainter until there was no further answer - although I knew she heard me still. At last, I knelt upon the floor and began to sing to her. My voice has no great merit, less even than my playing of the pianoforte, but she was always fond of it. For an hour, I sang through every favourite of hers that I could think of. At times she lay quietly with a slight smile upon her face. At others, she became animated, her eyes - though dimmed - would open suddenly wide and I could feel her joy. At last, I sang the one I knew she loved the very best of all. An expression of utter radiance broke across her face, she lifted her head a little from the pillow, I was yet holding her hand, and I brought it up to my face and held it against my cheek. Then she yawned, closed her eyes... her head dropped gently. For the briefest moment I believed she slept, but in that instant of passing I felt a deep, quick pulse in my heart and I knew...not that she was gone, but rather that she would be with me always - in the way that you know for sure what you never can explain, what never can be proven. It was like light, like love, as though all the true goodness inherent in each and every one of us, existed in that pulse. I knew too, from that moment, that there can be nothing ever to fear. That we leave our cares behind, but keep our loves. That we are here to grow, throughout our lives, as she did - and beyond. If you find this remembering too fanciful, I ask you to say nothing - for it is precious to me *(I share it with you knowing - hoping - you will treat it as the treasure that it is)*.

We were graced, this afternoon, by your Aunt and cousin who arrived unexpectedly by carriage, and for whom Mr Collins dragged nearly every piece of furniture from the parlour, to arrange at designated distances upon the lawn that his guests might sit and refuse tea for fear of polluted crockery. Each wore beautifully intricate masks which we were given to understand were painstakingly embroidered by Miss de Bourgh herself. Clearly, one may accomplish much during two hours of embroidering a day, although - as I conveyed quite firmly to your Aunt - I would not personally know, and have absolutely no intention of finding out. May I discreetly ask - do your Aunt and cousin truly believe it best to wear their masks below their noses? Mr Collins himself uttered a queried blunder in this direction, which was met first by frosty silence and then, after he had offered many compensatory bows and pulled his mask beneath his own proboscis, your Aunt at last declared that 'Anne finds her nasus greatly irritated by a mask, thus - clearly - it is best for all not to cover.' After many *subtle* gesticulations from Mr Collins, which we first professed not to comprehend, Charlotte and I also lowered our masks.

After an half hour, we were encouraged to go our own ways, leaving your Aunt and Mr Collins to discuss the improvements to Hunsford of your supposing. Your cousin was also there. Try as I might, I cannot seem to stop my mind from ruminating upon what they will be. Masks below the nose for everyone, I imagine. Outdoor visiting rights, perhaps? Although that may be still an aristocratic privilege. Perhaps the village might gather within their gardens, wearing masks as aforesaid, and stand mutely without food or drink while Mr Collins speaks. Oh, yes - that would be Sunday.

I was sorry indeed to see your cousin once more subdued. I had lately formed a rather different picture of her in my mind. I trust that, as you suggest, she is simply biding her time.

Charlotte and I took the opportunity to have a quiet walk together, our first since the edict, Maria being still indisposed - although a little better, thank you. It was all the more pleasant for being unexpected and long hoped for. Charlotte, it transpires, is more greatly concerned than I realized by her husband's ongoing feud with our Rochester-neighbours. 'Whilst wishing to be a good wife,' she told me 'I had not considered truly what might be required of me. Thus far, I had thought to let him have his way as much as possible, for the harmony of our relations. Now I wonder if I have rather wronged him instead. For the sake of a moment's peace, I have allowed him continuance along an imprudent path which, while clearly evident to me, was not so to him.'

She is in rather an impossible position.

Yours etc.

P.S. In answer to your question, it is not a 'Tattle Paper,' specifically. I believe this may be a name given by another. Early in lockdown, my Aunt Phillips had certainly assembled a copied sheet of news, and a scheme that this may be forwarded - once read - to (designated) others within the village. Why do you ask?

P.P.S. Respectfully, I do not recall referring to 'wives' regarding unpaid labour. Only Mrs Collins.

P.P.P.S. *My* Mr Collins! Why, that really is the worst of all.

Letter Twenty-four

Tuesday 9th June, Rosings Atrium of Archetypal Alteration

Dear Madam,

I could wish for the ability to convey within a letter my tone and therefore my intent, for both may be so easily misread. I required no apology, although I do thank you. Also, for the description of your Grandmama, which I shall treasure indeed.

I hope I have given no offence regarding the miscommunication received regarding your Aunt Phillips. News is greatly different to tattle. I assure you those were not my words. I enquired after - I confess - many weeks' hesitation - simply to have the information disproved or clarified by one whose testimony I trust. I am now satisfied.

I may only offer apology for my Aunt's unexpected visit. As I am sure you know by now, it was hardly out of character. I believe my Aunt intends to visit all within the parish over the next several weeks 'out of necessity' *(or belligerence)*. I am reliably informed that such a freedom is not, however, extended to me. I wonder, however, whether any or each of us may be welcome at any time in the future, after Sunday's sermon.

I took notes on the day, that we might enjoy its content again. To my slight shame, I was subject to my Aunt's approving eye for so doing, supposing that I did so out of admiration. Although generally I disapprove dissembling of any kind, under some circumstances it does appear essential; especially as a guest whose welcome has long been over-strained. Thus, I felt it best not to enlighten her.

To begin with an encouraging aspect, Mr Collins was acoustically faultless. Even without the Lady Catherine, his voice rang out far and wide. I had no previous suspicion of his ability to achieve such volume and clarity. My Aunt was truly delighted by his performance. Naturally, she was quite markedly alone in this, but cared not - a security which stems from an unassailable belief in the divine right of de Bourgs. Thankfully, her intentions for reform do not stem from a desire to extract unreasonable sums of money from those less fortunate than she, but more from a sustained assurance that whatever she believes best should be instantly adopted by all beneath her. Namely, everyone.

'Quintessential and Universal Reformatory Improvements for <u>All</u> Residents of Hunsford,

Without Exception and To Take Immediate Effect' (the title alone).

First, to remedy a quite alarming lapse in personal care, almost the entire populace being quite unforgivably grubby and dishevelled, residents are to bathe once a week, wash daily, brush their hair, wash their clothes, clean their shoes, sponge their teeth in brandy (an old idea, favoured by my Aunt), the use of birch or liquorice as an alternative, if they must. Boils to be lanced and, my particular favourite, all - again without exception - to eat less, that their clothing may better fit.

Gardens to be immediately maintained. Then, dwellings to be cleaned from top to bottom, clothes and bedding laundered and aired (the order specifically suiting my Aunt, who has been displeased during her daily drives to see gardens turned all to wildernesses).

Drowning spirits in potent portables to be frowned upon. Uplifting spirits instead through the partaking in regular exercise, the reading of suitable material - an approved list to be provided by the Rev. Collins - and the playing of instruments, if suitably proficient.

Wholesome games within the family may be allowed, but no wagers of any kind - lottery tickets and whist to be immediately banned. Ah, yes, quilting to be adopted by some, knitting or crocheting by others, dependent upon standing within the village. I do hope this latter does not apply to me.

With spirits as they have been, we are fortunate there was not a riot.

Regarding the use of masks, a demonstration given by Mr Collins as to how best to wear same (under the nose). Also, a demonstration to show that one should not wear a mask around one's neck, one's ear, one's ankle, or, indeed, one's arm. It may here be noted that I have witnessed no such infractions, but clearly my Aunt and ~~your~~ Mr Collins, believe it necessary to cover all possible contraventions.

Next, while Mr Collins (and Lady Catherine) appreciate that many may not understand the specific distance of seven feet, designated by the government for social distancing, he would be delighted to offer a demonstration for each and every member of the parish (demonstration then performed amidst bafflement, especially as clearly underestimated).

Finally, any with produce to sell may do so now on alternate Friday afternoons, with due care taken to adhere to all aforementioned measures. Coinage must be cleansed in lavender water before exchange, no exceptions.

The detached congregation did well throughout, I felt. In retrospect, it would have been better, perhaps, for Mr Collins to cease while ostensibly ahead. As it was, I was able to take only few notes concerning his consecutive lecture calling for greater decency in unmarried women, as the disruption in the - no doubt - already fraught crowd, drowned out all he had to say. Indeed, so potent and unified was their wailed chanting of 'my artichokes, oh, my dear artichokes,' that it took until late this morning for the echo to entirely leave my head. Evidently, news of Mr Collins's renegade goats has somehow spread, in spite of isolation.

I do hope that Miss Lucas is now much improved. My cousin noted her absence on Sunday and, I believe, has sent a recuperation gift via Mr Collins.

As soon as ever I hear more from Colonel Fitzwilliam, I shall let you know. As you suggest, news of our loved ones is also long overdue.

Yours etc.

P.S. Regarding Mrs Collins, you are right. She has my sympathy concerning the dilemma inherent in raising an unwitting indiscretion with one unlikely ever to take kindly to comment, no matter how well intended.

P.P.S. Regarding *'your* Mr Collins,' I can only wholeheartedly apologise.

Letter Twenty-five

Wednesday 10th June, Hunsford House of Convenient Protocols

Dear Sir,

Does any one of us take kindly to comment, I wonder? However well intended. I know of none who - while politely accepting a kindly-meant critique publicly, do not privately bite upon a chair and think the person wholly untruthful in private. We must all take our own part first, yes?

It is most generous of you to call Mr Collins's most recent indiscretion 'unwitting.' I could think of another word, similar, but with different meaning, which might better apply *(witless)*. Mind you, I confess I have a firm intent myself for a new leaf. It may not be entirely possible, whilst I share a lodging with... my cousin, but for the future I should like to say to everyone 'you did your best' or 'do what you will.' And mean it. Even Mr Collins. It is somewhat uncomfortable to be so censorious, even in jest. That being said, I am seldom so in as widespread or extreme a fashion as our respective relations were on Sunday morning. But there, I excuse myself again, as if I have no responsibility for my thoughts and words. I am grateful to have no pulpit, nor inclination towards.

My sister Jane has the best heart of any person I have ever known. She speaks no ill of anyone, and always speaks as she sees. At times I fear for her meeting with misuse in the world, but then I remind myself that her goodness will always attract like, her loving nature, love *(in time!)*.

'Let that be an end to it, my dear,' said Charlotte gently to her husband, as we reached the house. He nodded slightly. I do sincerely hope by that he will abide - even considering the continuing presence of the bathtub effigy. Although I was at first amused by Mr Collins's oration, it became truly painful to see him humiliated to such degree; and yet, he made his private grievances a matter for public consumption, so it was no wonder. Life is fraught with complication. Too far in one direction and the opposite thought comes to meet one in most compelling fashion. I pitied my cousin, for what he had created. It went too far too fast, and he was quickly overmuch immersed for clarity or, indeed, reasonability. Now he must rise up again on Sunday next, knowing most certain now that a cassock and the patronage of your Aunt will not ensure respect. I believe Charlotte intends in future to assist her husband in his sermon-writing. I know my friend well, and the set of her mouth indicates a firm purpose to intervene.

Maria is much improved, I thank you. She did indeed receive a rather beautiful paintbox from Miss de Bourgh and was utterly delighted by the attention. I know Charlotte and I are most grateful for the diversion it has given her. She is of a gentle and impressionable disposition and thus the perfect vicarious correspondent to Lydia's written escapades, for she is both suitably shocked and horribly compelled all at once.

I am not offended by your question regarding my Aunt Phillips, I wondered only from whence - of a sudden - it came. Indeed, in this case, perhaps, news and tattle are close relations. To give an *(unasked for)* explanation, my Aunt considers her role within the town as 'Merchant of Information' to be of great import. While she is, perhaps, sometimes ill-advised *(or indiscriminate)* in the news which she conveys, she is most conscientious in her visits and many are relieved of loneliness by her presence and inquisitive exuberance. Thus, in an awareness of present and ongoing isolation within the parish, she has taken it upon herself to continue in her duties. As far as I am given to understand, once a week my Aunt amasses news upon a sheet of paper - both sides. This she copies out five times and personally delivers to five households on an approved list. Once read, these households each convey their copy to another previously stipulated home, and so on and so forth until the sheets return to her. Each household is invited to add approving comments, should they wish; in fact, it is most decisively encouraged. If the militia are at all aware, they must surely turn a blind eye; perhaps because spirits are truly lifted by her efforts, or, more likely, because they realize it would be folly to try to stop her. The only matter not really to her credit, as I understand it, is that if even mildly offended by anyone within her circulation, they are suddenly - and without warning - removed from the list. Although I would not accuse my Aunt of deliberately looking for offence, she certainly does seem to discover it easily enough.

Goodness, it is warm, is it not? We are all in hiding. I write even later than usual, that I might sit undistracted in the cool.

Question: how does one cease to feel anger, whilst still believing it just? How does one forgive? How may one release the essentialness of being right, and in letting go of that, must one then be wrong? Why are we so afraid to feel we have erred, even slightly, that we will insist upon right and perpetuate something that might have faded long ago? Why are we so fearful of blunder, when our blunders are a necessary part of who we are, part of our growth?

Which leads me neatly to another query, which you may well refuse to answer, that being your right. I have it on reasonably good authority... well, authority, no. I have it from Mr Collins that Lady Catherine has suffered an 'a most grievous and quite outrageous outburst' from her nephew?

Can this be true?

Can this be you?

Yours etc.

P.S. Since writing the early part of this letter, I have heard from Charlotte that her husband has already completed another sermon - without her proffered assistance - on the subject of oppressors and the oppressed. He being victim, of course. Energised by outrage, he has also been out at all hours, digging a ditch around the perimeter of his estate, that 'trespassing neighbours' might swiftly tumble 'neck and crop.' We do not have the heart to tell him that the rope from the goats' pen was clearly easily removed by a long arm or crook reached through the hedge, without need for a toe to touch upon his grounds. Watching him at work, it strikes me as quite astonishing what may be achieved through vehement indignation, and remarkable how futile it frequently transpires to be.

P.P.S. Charlotte is to sell her goat's milk soap at Lady Catherine's market tomorrow. Maria and I are not to assist, as it would be 'inappropriate, indecent and unfitting.' Mr Collins concocts rules as swiftly and conveniently as my sister Mary does superstitions. It is a matter of private amusement to me to consider that every 'official' rule by which we are asked to abide was originally invented by some person or other. Often for the good of all. Sometimes for the good of only them. Imagine if, in four hundred or five hundred years' time, female descendants of Mr Collins are still to do (or not to do) all manner of silly things, just because *he* once said so. Thus, we must always think, before we pass something down.

Letter Twenty-six

Friday 12th June, Rosings Rooms of Musing Contemplation

Dear Madam,

Your question is one which I have frequently asked of myself, but I have yet to find a determined answer. When feeling, as you say 'just cause,' I have found that over time and with due diversion, my anger naturally abates, my *cause* becomes less insistent. Yet if circumstance draws my unmastered attention once more towards those I consider perpetrator, I discover all again, almost as if no time has passed. I would conquer this, for I feel it an aspect of my character which places me at tremendous disadvantage. To be so rapidly affected by events long passed is to find oneself continually weakened by that which may not be changed and, as you correctly observed in previous correspondence, how might we be certain that we remember justly? There is a state of mind open to all of us, from which no good can come; and anger gathers fuel as it is fed. I would surmount it, be master of myself, if I knew how.

I have finally submitted to the grooming of my locks, and Mr Shakespeare's beard has gone. I half miss it. My face seems strange to me now.

Having decreed that Anne's conjectural expedition to Coventry is at an end, and having rearranged every item (and person) which she - at present - may, my Aunt has taken to amusing herself by calling her daughter constantly and throughout the day, from the foot of the grand staircase. This is something of an annoyance, not only to Anne - whose responses grow increasingly irritable - but to those who room nearby. Being Her Ladyship, the summoning does not stop until Anne makes an appearance - at the very least at the top of the stairs - better yet, as close as possible to where my Aunt is standing. Naturally it is done out of a continuing insistence upon authority. But, as Mrs Norris knows, one may overcook anything.

'Never fear,' muttered Anne to me, upon a recent descent. 'When this is over, I plan to commit a minor felony and be transported to the new world.' Adding firmly, 'doubt it not.'

It is always good to have a clear objective.

I have, I believe, rather heartening news, having heard once more from the Colonel, although -

unfortunately - without, as yet, a reply which I might forward on to you. The anticipated protest took place last afternoon, commencing in St Giles - and moving west. Only forty marched, each masked, each holding extended - ahead and aside - either end of a broom, to ensure a good distance from one another as they walked. The Colonel tells that all walked in silence, without slogans or cries for change. When they reached the Green Park, they presented a scroll of paper on which was written the names of all who had been lost to hunger, all to fear, and sorrow. This was calmly received, and the men and women allowed to go upon their way. The Colonel - who seems deeply moved by the whole experience - states that this appears to have been all the more effective for being so greatly unexpected. Whoever led must be really quite remarkable.

I agree completely regarding the handing down of laws unchecked. Also, furniture. At Pemberley we have quite the most unfortunate set of cabinets which have been horrible heirlooms for several generations. Although no one within my family enjoys them, they are not to be disposed of, nor even placed out of sight. It is written. I do not understand it, yet - as their current owner - I have not the heart to be rid of them.

I can assure you that reports of my 'grievous outburst' have been grossly exaggerated. I simply - and gently - requested that Lady Catherine allow the village to go on as they pleased for a while, that Anne be free to pass her time as *she* thinks best, and that if my Aunt still wishes to impart wisdom to anyone, then Mr Collins might - as a willing candidate - be advised to treat everyone (cats included) with greater consideration. Finally, I asked that we all be released at last from this quite ridiculous dietary regime. I might add that at no point did I raise my voice, or employ a tone that was other than completely reasonable; though the thought of another portion of Pease soup was a fearsome provocation. Not one of my requests was accepted, and I felt no better for their airing. Thus, it goes.

Yours etc.

P.S. Mrs Collins's behaviour does her credit indeed. To be neither a fury on her husband's behalf, nor a fury towards her husband, is deeply admirable.

P.P.S. Your description of your elder sister aligns with what I too observed, an equality of consideration with all she meets.

P.P.P.S. Proprietary as she may be, I am not convinced of my Aunt's appreciating the idea of a market named in her honour.

Letter Twenty-seven

Monday 15th June, Hunsford Shelter for Truculent Clerics

Dear Sir,

I must offer a hasty correction to my words regarding my sister *(or perhaps your interpretation of such)*. Jane's sentiments are emphatically not of absolute equality with all. She has a true, affectionate heart, this is quite correct. However, although she is generous and amiable with all whom she meets, there is a deep wellspring of feeling reserved for her family and certain very particular others *(other)*. She may not be indiscriminately expressive of such with these particulars *(particular)*, but she is, I feel, all the better and truer for such lack of extravagance.

I am delighted - even amazed - to hear of so temperate a protest, especially when under such duress. It seems progress indeed. To have so profound an impact through so gentle and calm an undertaking is entirely admirable. Beyond admirable. I wonder now, what is to follow?

On the other end of the broom, as it were, I need not go into details of Mr Collins's sermon on oppression yesterday. You were there. Surplus food was thrown; the target attained with formidable accuracy. To see him upon the floor of his study afterward, propped against a wall, why, I confess to an experience of absolute compassion for the man, sunk now so low. I do not believe he has been allowed a thought of his own in his entire life. Every action he commits is, in truth, on behalf of another, to impress and ingratiate himself. In spite of tremendous speeches to the contrary, he seems to have absolutely no internal perception of his own value, believing such to be wholly dictated by how he is externally perceived.

Consequently, in what may only be described as a state of utter imbalance, and at the time unbeknown to we who were all abed, Mr Collins stumbled out late last night with his storm lantern and made his way in the direction of our Rochester-neighbours' home, with what objective only heaven knows. He now declares his intention to have been to go and 'have it out' with the head of their household, and remind him that _he_, as preacher, knew best for his flock, or something of the sort. Indeed, it was a challenge to comprehend his words. All the candles being out within, he hesitated next the old ash tree in the garden, to relieve his feelings, we think, he was reluctant to say. After this momentary pause, he decided to proceed, but - forgetting - tumbled headfirst into his own ditch, flinging the lantern upwards as he went. On its descent, it instantly caught the hedge alight. By the time all were awakened and water procured and thrown (how grateful I shall be not to have to draw from a pump ever, ever again), the entire perimeter hedgerow was gone, not to mention the goat enclosure, the goats being removed to safety by Maria and Charlotte at the earliest opportunity. Now there is not only nothing to stand as physical barrier between Mr Collins and his neighbours, but he is also at the mercy of their goodwill to believe the fire an accident.

That Mr Collins began the feud is undeniable. That his neighbours have continued it is also quite correct. Where will it end? What must yet occur for one party or other to call it over, when each have gone too far? How does one respond to such as my cousin - without becoming almost like him? Certain he is a man of decided patterns of behaviour, so regular in his thoughts, so determined in his righteousness, that any event out of the ordinary throws him into a chaos of letters and sermons in an attempt to control what he may not. He does not intend any cruelty, I believe that. He has simply been raised never to question what once was learnt. But there, you see, I attempt to understand him, when I may only understand myself. Is the answer simply to go one's own way, as if he does not exist? That in no longer attempting to persuade him otherwise, one is able to release oneself from the awful need to have him be something beyond his reach? And yet, the fire is an all too cogent expression... of what? He is often foolish, frequently witless, daily careless, but never a man to commit a physically destructive action such as that.

Thus, it remains for his neighbours to decide which way to proceed. Do they persist in painful acrimony, loathing Mr Collins not just for what has transpired, but for what might have happened had the night gone ill (or iller)? We are all faced with such choices at one time or another. Do we continue to think poorly of another, to frighten ourselves at 'evil-intent,' rather than to think it simply petty foolishness, or an unfortunate lack of foresight? Do we proceed along a path where only further misery for all awaits? Tell each of our acquaintance of the wrong done to us, exaggerating a little as our reach extends? Or do we stop, while we can, bear our parts as best we may, then move forward graciously, knowing better what we would have in the world, what we would be?

I confess, I like the Rochester-neighbours. There is something buoyant and joyful about them. I have every faith in their forgiveness.

It must be a relief to have your Aunt once more verbally engaging with her daughter. Mama frequently ceases to speak to, well, most of us, at one time or another. But never for an entire week. Actually, she seldom manages more than an afternoon before she forgets herself and resumes communication - and that is only supposing that during that afternoon we, or she, is away from home. Otherwise, she is speaking again within moments.

There is something in the air, at present (other than the Unmentionable) for Maria of all people has this day had at Mr Collins. I think she took her chance having seen him so humbled after the fire. For this I cannot blame her; she has borne through the last few months with barely a whimper of complaint concerning her new brother. I was not there and did not hear, but - as I understand it - she presented him an itemised page of frustrations, front and back. To hint that he did not receive it well would be a quite colossal understatement. In history, it is ever thus - a small group of people, often related, at loggerheads.

On that theme, I offer humble apology for dubbing the Hunsford Market in honour of your Aunt, it was most inappropriate of me. From what I understand, it was a very quiet affair and poorly attended. I suspect the additional provisions anticipated for sale had been set by to throw at Mr Collins in the future.

Yours etc.

P.S. Could you consider gifting the cabinets to someone of whose friendship you would rid yourself? My father was given a ring by a Great Great Aunt who found him 'insubordinate and troublesome.' Having few fond memories of the lady, he one day presented the ring to my Mama, in the first year of their marital bliss. She was most underwhelmed. 'Why you should think I would be delighted by some old relic is quite beyond me, Mr Bennet,' she declared - she tells the story herself to this day. 'Why, supposing I wear this and then am destined to live the same life as the personage who owned it first? I would not wish that under any circumstances.' She was vastly less impressed when she discovered a lock of the lady's hair within the ring, of which Papa had been - hitherto - unaware. My father, on the other hand, was rather gratified and keeps the ring yet, comprehending in the gift a fondness of which he had been previously unaware.

P.P.S. The awful irony that while in London so many go hungry, but in Hunsford food is thrown, is not lost upon me.

Letter Twenty-eight

Wednesday 17th June, Rosings Bastion of Filial Fortitude

Dear Madam,

Colonel Fitzwilliam returned this evening, quite exhausted, but in a humour of the most tremendous relief and optimism also. He sat within the dining room for the briefest period, supping quietly while we three inmates looked on, suppressing a thousand questions. Even my Aunt remained quiet, a handkerchief pressed to her lower face. It seems the Colonel has had little recent opportunity for sleep; or indeed a bath. We are all deeply curious to hear fully of his experiences, but must restrain ourselves a little longer while he recovers. He was abed before the first candle was lit.

I sincerely regret that we at Rosings knew nothing of the parsonage fire, for we would have offered every possible aid. Thank heaven it was no worse. You must instruct me as to whatsoever I might offer by way of assistance or appeasement. Having laughed at the side-lines, I cannot deny my part in the co-creation of this... spectacle.

Speaking from my own experience*... No, I may not... In the case of this manifestation, it was clearly commenced as a simple exchange of insult for insult, mounting in recklessness and severity. Mr Collins began it, no question, and without reasonability, rationality or benevolence on his side; but with my Aunt instead, which doubtless felt the same to him. Reprisal followed, humorous as it was. Had he not felt such pride and righteousness in his post, he might have stopped. Had your neighbours not retaliated... he would certainly have continued anyway. What, then, were they to do? Or anyone when faced with such absurdity and intolerance? Mr Collins has surely been directed along this path since he was old enough to walk. Try as I may, I cannot solve it, unless we are to shut him away for a year and bombard him with alternative configurations of thought? But then, and without doubt, he would resent such an action grievously and simply bide his time to return to old behaviour with even greater verve and vendetta.

From personal experience... But, no. I cannot... I might only say that I have found myself *wishing* to excuse another, *believing* I had done so, only to find my trust once more and soon betrayed. Yet, may I truly, objectively, speak of forgiveness? Did I indeed, in actuality, set out to forgive? Or did I simply offer dismissal; a weary, weakened trust and then lie in wait, certain of its being broken? In attempt to guard ourselves from further hurt, do we simply dig more pits wherein distress dwells?

It does appear that Mr Collins lacks the truest freedom of all - to think as one will. When so much from our earliest years is under the scrutiny of others, to find, yet, that still, quiet place of private truth, of particular preferences, is of paramount importance, and must be constantly reached for as something attainable by all.

Indeed, coincidentally, such has been the subject of recent lengthy consideration on my part; in light of what I have witnessed at Rosings, my own - more personal - experiences at both school, the university and at home, and the intense relief that finding myself unable to look at a newspaper has given me. Aware as I was, that whatsoever I was reading had been constructed by another human being, and therefore influenced by their own particular point of view, however impartial their intentions, I confess to finding myself still deeply, often most unfortunately, influenced by aught to which I gave my attention; with the added vexation of little true power to offer assistance or alteration in each depicted circumstance. I was often angered, at the very least frustrated. Seldom to any purpose.

If all might keep to their own trust, could each then - more readily - let one another be? Or is the interest and engagement we have with one another part of the rich pageantry of this life? Each answer offers only more questions.

It seems that Mr Collins is now known locally as the Prince Regent.

It amused me to hear of your Mama's attempts at silence with her offspring. I could sincerely wish my Aunt might be so unsuccessful. She has taken, recently, to calling Anne 'an oddity.' Also 'strange' and 'distinctly mad.' That word, once more. To the last, Anne suggested - quite calmly, I would add - that she might seek employment for herself as a governess or chamber maid, thus securing a lasting independence from her mother. The horror at her daughter lowering herself to such, and thus lowering the name of de Bourg, was enough to render my Aunt pale and without retort. Anne was quite delighted.

Yours etc.

P.S. I can think of several who might enjoy said cabinets. An excellent suggestion, thank you. Perhaps we might part with them after all.

P.P.S. Regarding Anne once more, you may be interested to know that she and Mrs Norris have formed an alliance. Whether it is friendship or not, I may not speculate. Certain, there is trade. Anne - unlike my shamed self - noticed that Mrs Norris alone was left to wash for the household without assistance. Although most are altering attire less than usual, it is - as you once observed - a considerable task, especially for one. That we might have extra and more tasty rations without my Aunt's knowledge, Anne has offered help, for which Mrs Norris appears sincerely grateful. My Aunt is, thankfully, yet to notice the state of Anne's knuckles. I have considered offering my own assistance, but readily admit no inclination towards such. Thus, if I am asked, then I shall roll up my sleeves - but not until.

Letter Twenty-nine

Thursday 18th June, Hunsford Parsonage - A letter of Gratitude (Ultimately)

Dear Sir,

I can hardly contain my delight at receiving news of the Colonel's safe return. I confess, I am also deeply curious to hear his detailed report of the happenings in London *(and other matters*****)*. I wonder if he knows aught of whether quarantine might soon be at an end?

I find myself both patience and impatience personified. I have never known such a time of contrast. I am glad of it. If I allow it, allow the growth.

I have decided at last and after long deliberation that if I *were* able to effect one change in the world, it would be that all thought truly well enough of themselves to be sincerely happy. Imagine all the trouble it would save. From my observations, it seems clearly apparent that most of the 'bad' behaviour in the world could surely be credited to an abiding feeling of personal lack, satiable only by attempting to pull others along with you. I do not -

cannot - believe this to be congenital. It must surely be enforced, then perpetuated.

I have heard of Mr Collins's new moniker and while I confess it did amuse me, I do consider it slightly unfair. My cousin may be many things, but he is certainly not a profligate. Quite the opposite, in fact. Mr Collins himself heard of his new title this afternoon, and now accuses all and sundry of the most profound disloyalty. Including the goats.

Prior to this discovery, and - indeed - to his credit*(?)*, he attempted to make every amend within his power. A verbose and quite sincere apology from a proper seven foot away. Digging and clearing the remainder of the hedges and planting new ones, transposed from part of your Aunt's estate - and with your Aunt's *(withering)* permission - in the very cart by which his neighbours moved, not so long ago. We three women have baked and baked these last days, and all has been most graciously received. Your Aunt, as I understand it, is furious with her Clergyman. The greatest punishment imaginable for the man.

It does strike me repeatedly that our new neighbours are predominantly joyful people, and that Mr Collins - in all truth – is not. I wonder, did he set about their reformation out of a genuine belief that they required reform, or, because he in some way wished them to be less happy, that his own lack of joy could be less evident. In which case, what foolishness to turn all his attention *towards* them, rather than away.

On the subject of penance, Maria's has now begun in less-amusing earnest. Charlotte was dispatched to arrange a room for her with a trusted woman in the village, that her husband may not be forced to see or hear from his sister again. He has decried it a spousal duty to remove from his presence any person whom he deems intolerable (quarantine or no) and is, it would appear, absolutely not to be persuaded otherwise. I am greatly surprised at the immediate compliance of both sisters. Maria is repentant at the 'trouble' she has 'caused' and anxious to go quietly, although I do believe this to stem – in partiality – from an irresistible sense of ensuing freedom. Charlotte is resigned, even hardened to her present course. During our very brief discourse on the subject, Charlotte intimated that she has faith in her husband's wrath being short-lived. I am less convinced. Indeed, I confess to feeling deeply unsettled by the course Mr Collins insists upon for Maria, for Charlotte, and for the entire Lucas family, if this really is allowed to perpetuate. Perhaps I am overly mistrustful, but it bodes ill that having caused so much offence himself, he would then make so little effort at reparation, allow for none on the part of Maria, and hold the sibling bond to be of so little value. It feels almost as if he has found an excuse to be rid of her; although I cannot imagine why he should wish it. Yet, if Maria is pardoned within a score of years I shall be deeply, deeply shocked.

You have my agreement - as tempting as it may seem, if you were to shut Mr Collins away and engage him with newer, warmer ideas, he would simply resist with all his might, deeming them false and wicked. We all are prone to frequent blunders. Perhaps the desire truly and universally inherent is to reclaim clarity within - or to simply feel... better! I have no doubt that Mr Collins's anger is really more intense towards himself than to anyone else, for all the bluff and *(ahem)* smoke. If he might allow himself an error or... ten, accept this as natural and that our growth is of more value than all else, then step forward afresh, knowing more firmly where best to tread - would this not be a conciliation of a kind?

We are not meant to drag the past behind us. It is too heavy. The more we chew on our wrongs and woes, the more they trouble us. What if we grew more skilled at leaving them aft? Ah, how freely and freshly we might skip through life, were it not for what *she* had said or *he* had done twenty year ago!!

As if oblivious to familial upheaval, my testing cousin has found the time to create a device, constructed of a tiny, hinged mallet, and a small piece of wood, which, when brought together, creates a resonant and repetitive rapping sound. With this he attempts – several times a day - to call the free cat to his will. There can be few undertakings, I imagine, more futile than the attempt to train a cat. Thus, he has simply conceived yet another device with which to infuriate himself. Charlotte has suggested that a place in the garden is constructed, especially for him, where he might go and spend an ample portion of his time in peaceful contemplation. Sheltered, of course, for the winter months. He is persuaded that this will be a good and healthful thing for him. Also, a new enclosure for the goats.

I am all amazement to hear of the bourgeoning friendship between your cousin and Mrs Norris. The Unmentionable makes for the most unlikely of fellowships. I was under the impression that Mrs Norris was supported by three other members of staff. Are all now dismissed?

Yes indeed – Mad - *that* word again. Just three letters and so easy to use regarding another without care or forethought. I hold yet that it is employed as a distraction by those who cause the most terrible pain to the accused and refuse to account for it, even privately.

We all deserve a second venture; I do believe that. A multitude of ventures. Our misconception is that these must be bestowed upon us by others, rather than gifted by ourselves. Every day is a new opportunity. Every moment. If we are sensitive, we know when a situation does not feel right to us. Must we remain confined, standing by old decisions that no longer serve? Or do we heed the call, do better next time, according to our own true nature? When we stay for the endorsement of others, or even their forgiveness, we often find ourselves in a limbo of sorrow, not understanding - perhaps - that others may only forgive and approve according to their own practised beliefs. Thus, it is no condemnation to remain unforgiven as it is simply an indication of another's progress through life, deserving only our brief compassion. We must look forward, reaching for life in all its fullness. We must allow one another to be human – even Mr Collins, and the Master of Paddles; and even if we find it best to leave them far, far behind.

These are the thoughts that cause me sleepless nights now. Sleepless nights! An entirely new concept.

I hope we are near the end of this... epoch. Valuable as it has been.

Yours etc.

P.S. Please remember me once more to the Colonel.

P.P.S. It is a strange fact of letter-writing, in a desire to amuse one becomes a bearer of tales, and as one knows 'tale-bearers are as bad as the tale-makers.' Within society, I simply ask questions and let others tell the tales. Within a letter, that will not do. I would emphasise - I am truly grateful for this time and for all I have learned... for our correspondence... to have found so willing a counterpart in my quest for amusement... I appreciate... but am eager - oh so eager - for life to return in all its vibrant richness.

P.P.P.S. On revisiting an earlier letter, I find I have a pressing question. Who was Hugh, and how and why did he come to have a Temple built in his honour?

Letter Thirty

Friday 19th June, Rosings Refuge of Reprehensible Aunts

Dear Madam,

Ah yes, the Hugh Temple of Peace. Well, I must confess, there was – as far as I know - no Hugh. It was a misunderstanding of mine from childhood. My father had told me of the vast temple's destruction, attempting to explain to my four-year-old self the meaning of 'vast' or 'huge.' It was many years before I realized my mistake, and I am now rather fond of the sobriquet.

Regarding the servants of your mentioning, they have indeed long-since departed. Two at the urgent request of Lady Catherine, and one of her own, equally pressing, volition.

I am powerless to offer solution concerning the unprecedented behaviour of Mr Collins with regard to Miss Lucas. I may only prospect that it arises as a consequence of these uncertain times and will, thus, be remedied in due course. Nothing on earth could induce me to behave so to my sister. It is quite simply beyond my comprehension.

I am obliquely put in mind of a second-cousin-twice-removed who would join us for the Christmas festivities when I was very young, Georgiana being not yet born. The man was partial to the imbibing of large quantities of liquid refreshment and, on each visit, there would unfailingly come a time when it seemed quite correct to him to tell my father and mother exactly what he thought of them. It was seldom complimentary. In the morning he would have no memory of the incident, leaving my parents at a loss as to how to respond to such persistent and unflattering indiscretion. His father, who generally accompanied him, suffered equally from fleeting amnesia or, if pressed, would become suddenly irate and accuse my parents of a 'deeply disappointing and selfish over-sensitivity' to his son's 'humour.' After the fourth occasion, my father took it upon himself to speak gently and sincerely to both. They left immediately and in high dudgeon, refusing all subsequent invitations.

Miss Lucas has always struck me as a mild, good-tempered person. If she tendered complaint, I do not doubt it was well-founded. Yet conscience compels me to proffer that her written-rebuke was a fraction ill-judged, especially considering her subject. If Mr Collins has proven anything over these past weeks it is that he is inherently, profoundly incapable of withstanding criticism, no matter how much he may personally distribute. We must not allow ourselves to become recriminatory puppets, however powerful the provocation.

―

My mother's cousin made a most unfortunate match. She was an exceptional woman, independent and full of spirit. Yet she married a man who was... unkind. Never in public. In fact - to this day - he remains largely revered. For many years my mother was her one confidant; naturally only by letter, for the lady in question was kept far apart from extended family and friends. In time, the frequency of the letters dwindled to once or twice a year. She lived in isolation, wandering the halls of their home, unable to remember her own name and, eventually, distanced from her daughter who, after countless attempts at assistance, could no longer bear to witness a circumstance of such sorrow without solution.

Do you know, I believe my Aunt not so dissimilar from her gracious subject as once I supposed? I wonder, have I been rather too blinded prior by an *awareness* of her 'nobility' to notice. Or perhaps our correspondence has shed some much needed - long-desired, even - light. For whatsoever her Ladyship most urges, flies - almost invariably - as swiftly as ever it can... away. She fights. She is used to fighting. She believes that conquest will give her what she wants, speaks proudly of being 'a Formidable Foe.' Yet when one examines carefully, it is never long before the latest tenacious passion slips once more from her grasp. I wonder that she cannot see. Lady Catherine is, I understand, widely feared, and - sadly - engenders the affection of few. Indeed, she does not allow affection, but, instead, demands it. An oxymoron.

I never considered my Aunt to be one for superstition, but she too has - of a sudden - acquired an unexpected penchant for assistance in warding off ill fortune. In this case, she has accused Anne of 'giving her the irksome eye,' and called upon a woman from the village to investigate her suspicions. I was not present for the rituals, but am given to understand that they involved clove-buds, a candle, and were inconclusive. Thus, she remains 'all a-jitter.'

'If I knew how, I would most certainly have done it,' murmured Anne.

My Mother once told me that Lady Catherine wished, many, many moons ago, to be a dancer - a Marie Sallé. It was not possible. My Uncle spent many, many years attempting to compensate for this loss. That was not possible either.

In truth, I cannot counter the irresistible inkling that my Aunt is almost certainly at the root of Mr Collins's decision regarding Miss Lucas. Lady Catherine requires almost constant intellectual stimulation and, in its absence, finds regrettable amusement for herself in fidgeting among the affairs of others.

Please forgive the open expression of my frustrations. I am steadily compiling my own itemised list, yet – taking heed of Miss Lucas – will have to make do with burning it, upon completion.

Of course, the origin of the word 'family' lies in the Latin 'familia,' which translates as 'household servants.' But I expect you know this.

―

Now to Colonel Fitzwilliam, and London. It pains me to relate that news arrived this morning to subvert his aforementioned humour and optimism. The peaceful protest of which we spoke was not, as initially thought, well received by the powers that be. Indeed, late last night, each protestor was taken from their home and all are now incarcerated, awaiting trial for 'the execution of an indisputable attempt to incite civil disruption.' Cover of darkness, naturally, had no effect upon the information reaching far and wide. Those who reported the original event factually are now documenting the injustice; those, less factual, herald the 'necessary protection of the public from dangerous insurgents.'

I confess, I have long wondered why quarantine was not implemented with swifter efficiency. Had they locked the ships down sooner, would all have transpired as it has? I am no stranger to wisdom in retrospect, yet this is hardly the first time in our nation's history that such a circumstance has occurred. How much misfortune might have been spared if, in the very first instance, the ships had immediately been held at anchor and lazarettos established? Do we employ the teachings of the past as well as we might? Grudges are held on to, but lessons remain unlearnt.

Yet while we might blame the government for what has been poorly managed, we give all external power to strangers, and not ourselves.

Know that I have more information than I am at liberty to disclose. Would that I could. As an extensive reader, like yourself (though you deny it) I have observed that in novels, as in life, responses to challenging events are generally rooted in these factors – a desire for power, a desire for love, for monetary gain, or a wish to be seen as hero or benefactor.

The existence of the Unmentionable is undeniable, yet in every trial of body and spirit there are those who will do their best to overcome, bring aid and as swift an end to suffering as possible, those who seek the greater good; and then those who seek personal advantage, personal gain, and are indifferent to the collateral destruction.

I would like to be of service in some way; observing now how much distress might surely have been spared with foresight. Yet I fear my own background of privilege is hardly conducive to sufficient understanding of the desperate plight of an existence rooted in poverty and deprivation. To live from hand to mouth, with the terrifying anxiety of knowing not how to provide from one day to the next… I may imagine, but that is not enough. Like the so called 'mad' women of previous discourse, are those in privation not additionally, in truth, quite deliberately stifled and diverted, for want of a better word, by the constant propagation of loss, of fear. Much of import may be ignored while chaos reigns. Thus, it is essential for each of us to question what we are told.

———

The Colonel has this instant informed me of his immediate departure once more to London, following an urgent communication.

A scandal has erupted in our parliament, our Primus Inter Pares betrayed by one he appeared to trust, the government in disarray and lockdown abruptly at an end. The Colonel has heard of a London in absolute confusion, almost the entire city taking to the streets in either celebration or protest. I must away directly. The Colonel has assured me that he will look to my sister's well-being as soon as ever he may, but I cannot leave this to him alone. Thus, I depart immediately and heaven help any who stand in my way.

We are not here to watch.

Yours etc.

P.S. I am now able, most belatedly, to enclose Colonel Fitzwilliam's reply to your urgent query. I do hope you find it satisfactory.

P.P.S: Please be assured of my swift return. I hope that I… may… call upon you… in the future. I hope…

Glossary

Are the trees in the field human, that they should be besieged by you?	Quoted from the Book of Deuteronomy 20:19
Asclepion	Referring to Healing Temples located in Ancient Greece.
Aurelius, Marcus	Roman emperor from 161 to 180 AD and a Stoic philosopher. 'Meditations' is a series of private reflections and ideas by Aurelius, never intended for publication.
Banbury Cakes	A spiced, currant-filled, flat pastry cake, made in the Banbury region to secret recipes since 1586 or earlier and still made there today.
Bastion	A fortress or stronghold.
Beauty patch	Known as 'plaisters' in England, covering scars and pockmarks. The French called them mouches (flies) as they resembled small insects. Often fanciful shapes, such as heart and stars.
Bennet, Elizabeth	The spirited protagonist of Jane Austen's Pride and Prejudice. Frequently known as Lizzy or Eliza by her friends and family. She is the second-eldest of the five Bennet sisters.
Bennet, Jane	The eldest Bennet sister. Beautiful and kind, she tends only to see the best in others. She falls in love

	with Charles Bingley, a rich young gentleman recently moved to Hertfordshire, but he is persuaded that she does not care for him and so, reluctantly, jilts her.
Bennet, Catherine 'Kitty'	The fourth Bennet sister, very much under the influence of her younger sister Lydia.
Bennet, Lydia	The youngest Miss Bennet; a tremendous flirt, careless of others, wilful and imprudent.
Bennet, Mary	The middle Bennet sister; earnest and studious.
Bennet, Mr	Lizzy's Papa, who feels tremendous affinity with his second-eldest daughter. Well-read, with a very dry wit, rather tired of his wife and younger daughters. His estate, Longbourn, is entailed to the male line.
Bennet, Mrs	Lizzy's Mama. Prone to nervous fits and tremors. Her entire focus is upon marrying off each of her daughters to wealthy men. Often heavy-handed and socially unskilled.
Bingley, Caroline	Mr Bingley's vain and snobbish sister who has set her sights on becoming the wife of Mr Darcy.
Bingley, Mr Charles	Darcy's close friend and suitor to Jane Bennet. Handsome, kind and wealthy, but easily persuaded away from his own true inclinations. Darcy has mis-

	observed Jane's modesty when around Bingley, assuming that it denotes a lack of feeling. He has used this to persuade his friend not to pursue his courtship.
Birthday celebration	Although Birthdays were marked during the Regency period, they were not celebrated as such. The King's Birthday would be widely celebrated, however, as a national holiday.
Blockhead	An idiot
Breeches	Breeches, or short pants, were worn just below the knee.
Brummel, Mr	George Bryan 'Beau' Brummell; a fashion icon of Regency England. For a time, close friend to the Prince Regent. (1778 - 1840)
Cassock	An ankle-length garment worn by members of the Christian Clergy.
Catalani, Angelica	An Italian opera singer (1780 - 1849) with an incredible three octave range, who performed at the King's Theatre, Haymarket, London 1806 - 1807.
Cheapside	A street in the historic and modern financial centre of the City of London.
Cheesecakes	Rather different to present-day cheesecakes, Regency ones were more akin to the modern Danish: a puff-pastry filled with custard.
Collins, Mrs Charlotte	Recent wife to Mr Collins, daughter to Sir William Lucas and

	Lady Lucas, and Lizzy's closest friend. At twenty-seven, believing her marital prospects to be hopeless, she agrees to marry Mr Collins, thus gaining financial security and relieving herself of the fear that she is a burden to her parents.
Collins, Mr William	Mr Bennet's distant second cousin, a clergyman, and the current heir to the estate of Longbourn House. He is a pompous, wearisome man, fawningly devoted to his patroness, Lady Catherine de Bourgh. On visiting Longbourn, he set his sights on marrying Jane Bennet, but finding she was soon to be engaged to Mr Bingley, proposed to Lizzy instead. When she rejected him, he proposed to Charlotte Lucas and was accepted.
Coryza	Catarrhal inflammation of the mucous membrane in the nose.
Coventry, expedition to	To send someone to Coventry is an English expression meaning to deliberately ostracise someone from their family or community. Typically, this is done by not talking to them, avoiding their company, and acting as if they no longer exist. This possibly originates from the English Civil War, when Royalist prisoners of

	war were taken to Coventry and then shunned by residents.
Dancing allowed for married couples	In Austen's time, dancing in public with your spouse - although not unheard of - was generally frowned upon.
Darcy, Fitzwilliam	The romantic hero of Pride and Prejudice. A wealthy man who owns a large estate in Derbyshire called Pemberley. Initially, he appears to be unpleasant and haughty, but - as the novel progresses - he is revealed to have a noble heart, capable of tremendous love and loyalty.
Darcy, Georgiana	Darcy's sister, younger by a decade. She is gentle and accomplished, with a dowry of £30,000. Mr Wickham persuaded her to elope with him when she was fifteen, but she was saved by the intervention of her brother.
De Bourg, Anne	The only child of the late Sir Lewis and Lady Catherine de Bourg. She is heir to the de Bourg estate, Rosings Park.
De Bourg, Lady Catherine	Aunt to Mr Darcy and Colonel Fitzwilliam. A difficult, controlling woman, used to having her own way.
Denny, Mr	An officer. Friend to Wickham and Lydia Bennet.
Fitzwilliam, Colonel	Nephew of Lady Catherine de Bourgh and Lady Anne Darcy

For aliens have entered the holy places of the Lord's house	(Darcy's mother); cousin to Anne de Bourgh and the Darcy siblings. Jeremiah 51:51
Forced Strawberries	Cultivating strawberries in a greenhouse/orangery for fruiting and consumption all year round, rather than for a season.
Fordyce, Rev James	A Scottish Presbyterian minister and poet, best known for his collection of sermons published in 1766, Sermons for Young Women, or Fordyce's Sermons. (1720 - 1796)
Gardiner, Aunt & Uncle	Mrs Bennet's brother and sister-in-law. He is a successful tradesman, which earns the scorn of Caroline Bingley, even though - or because - her own fortune comes from trade. Both he and his wife are kind and level-headed and close to their nieces Jane and Elizabeth.
Gracechurch Street	A main road in the historic and financial centre of the City of London. Home to the Gardiner Family.
Gray, Thomas	An English poet, letter-writer, classical scholar, and professor at Pembroke College, Cambridge (1716 - 1771). Lizzy is referring to

	his 'Ode on a Distant Prospect of Eton College.'
Gruel	A thinner type of porridge, consisting of cereal boiled in water or milk.
Grose, Francis - A Classical Dictionary of the Vulgar Tongue	A collection of rude words and slang, first published in 1785 by Francis Grose.
Head, Richard - The Canting Academy	A slang dictionary written in 1673.
History of Little Goody Two-Shoes, The	A children's story by John Newbery, published in 1765.
Hunsford	A Parsonage near Westerham and the home of Mr and Mrs Collins
Joseph as Vizier of Egypt	Gen 41:41-52. Joseph was betrayed into slavery by his jealous brothers, but rose to become appointed Vizier, the second most powerful man in Egypt, after the Pharaoh.
King, Mary	A minor character in Pride & Prejudice who inherits ten thousand pounds from a distant relative. She is courted by Mr Wickham and then taken out of harm's way to Liverpool by an Uncle.
Lazarettos	A quarantine station for maritime travellers. Can refer to ships permanently at anchor, isolated islands, or mainland buildings. The first lazaretto was established

	by Venice in 1423 on the island of Santa Maria di Nazareth in the Venetian Lagoon
Lea, The	The River Lea, also spelled Lee, originating in the Bedfordshire part of the Chiltern Hills, and flowing southeast through Hertfordshire and then Greater London.
Lind, James	A Scottish doctor and the pioneer of hygiene in the Royal Navy. By conducting clinical trials, he discovered that citrus fruits cured scurvy. (1716 - 1794)
Lock, stock and barrel	A popular saying for many centuries. Based on the three main components of a flintlock gun: lock denoting the firing mechanism, stock the wooden shoulder-piece to which it is attached, and barrel, the conduit through which the bullet is fired.
Longbourn	Hertfordshire residence of The Bennet Family.
Lottery tickets	A game of chance played with cards/tickets and fish/tokens.
Lucas Lodge	Hertfordshire residence of the Lucas Family.
Lucas, Maria	Younger sister to Charlotte (Lucas) Collins, sister-in-law to Mr Collins and daughter of Sir William and Lady Lucas.

Lucas, Sir William & Lady	Neighbours and friends to The Bennet family.
Sallé, Marie	A French dancer and choreographer, famous in the 18th century for her emotive, dramatic performances. (1707 - 1756)
Mad as Old King George	Referring to George III, father to George IV. In later life, he suffered from frequent periods of mental illness, leading to the establishment of a Regency in 1810. (1738 - 1820)
Master of Ceremonies	Responsible for supervising every aspect of a ball, from room arrangements and adherence to dress codes, to musicians and the order of dances. He would also introduce prospective dancing partners to one another.
Master of Paddles	Nickname for the Master of Ceremonies by Lizzy.
Master of Punting	Nickname for the Master of Ceremonies by Darcy.
Meryton	A fictional town in Pride & Prejudice, located near Longbourn and Netherfield in Hertfordshire.
Miasma	Bad air, or night air. A now obsolete theory that diseases were caused by a miasma, imparted from decaying organic matter.

Militia	A military force of civilians, raised to supplement the regular army in case of emergency.
Multum stercora in parvum spatium	Translates roughly as 'a lot of rubbish in a small space.'
Nasus	Latin for nose.
Neck and crop	Originally used to describe a spectacular fall from a horse where the unseated rider flies past the horse's neck and throat, crop being an archaic word for throat. Came to mean 'entirely, completely.'
Pantry	A small room or cupboard in which food, crockery, and cutlery are kept.
Pay your taxes	A cheeky reference to the fate of Aristocrats during the French revolution, who were largely exempt from paying taxes. It is suggested that Darcy is a member of the old Anglo-Norman aristocracy, as indicated by his own name and that of his Aunt, Lady Catherine de Bourgh, although he does not possess a title.
Pease-soup	Also known as Pease pudding and Pease porridge, it's a savoury dish made of boiled legumes, typically split yellow peas, with water, salt, and spices, often cooked with a bacon or ham joint.

Pemberley	Derbyshire estate owned by Fitzwilliam Darcy.
Phillips, Aunt	The sister of Mrs. Bennet and Edward Gardiner, and Aunt to the Bennet and Gardiner children. She is widely thought to be rather vulgar.
Piano Forte	A fortepiano is an early piano dating from around 1700 to the early 19th century. During Pride & Prejudice, Lady Catherine states to Lizzy of music that 'there are few people in England, I suppose, who have more true enjoyment of music than myself, or a better natural taste. If I had ever learnt, I should have been a great proficient. And so would Anne, if her health had allowed her to apply.' She encourages Mrs Collins to play the piano forte in Mrs Jenkinson's room (Anne's companion in the novel) where she will be in 'nobody's way.'
Polemoscope	An opera glass or field glass with an oblique lens and side aperture that allows the user to discretely see what is happening to their left or right. Known also as 'Jealously Glasses.'
Pontius	Referring to Pontius Pilate, fifth governor of Judaea 26/27 to 36/37 AD, under Emperor Tiberius. Well-known today as the

	official presiding over the trial of Jesus. In Matthew's 27:24, Pilate, 'seeing that he was getting nowhere, but that a riot was starting instead' took some water and 'washed his hands in front of the crowd, and said, 'I am innocent of this man's blood. See to it yourselves!''
Portent	A sign or warning that a momentous event is likely to happen.
Potent portables	Alcoholic beverages.
Pottle	A sort of conical basket used to carry produce.
Poultice	A soft, moist cloth, containing herbs, bran or flour, which, when applied to the body, relieves soreness and inflammation.
Primus Inter Pares	Latin: a first among equals. The Prime Minister.
Prince Regent, The	Later George IV. The eldest son of King George III and Queen Charlotte. From 1811 until his accession, he served as Regent during his father's final illness. He was known among the people as a profligate, thanks to a careless and extravagant lifestyle. (1762 - 1830)
Quizzing Glass	A single magnifying lens on a handle, held up before the eye to enable close scrutiny of an object or person.

Greene, Robert	A prolific English author and dramatist, who enjoyed popularity during his lifetime. 'The Black Bookes Messenger' details the villainies of one Ned Browne. Today, he is best known for a pamphlet believed to be an attack on William Shakespeare entitled 'Greene's Groats-Worth of Witte, bought with a million of Repentance.' (1558 - 1592)
Rosings	The palatial dwelling of Lady Catherine de Bourgh, located in Kent. Hunsford Parsonage - home of the Collinses - shares one of its boundaries.
Sanctioned by Papa	While Lizzy's Mama is adamant that her daughter accepts Mr Collins's proposal in order that the entailed estate of Longbourn may remain within the family, her Papa allows that the match does not go ahead, appreciating just how much it would be against Lizzy's wishes.
Scandal Sheets	A newspaper or magazine specializing in scandalous stories or gossip.
Sesquipedalian	A long and ponderous word, polysyllabic.
Shakespeare & Goldsmith both agree	Shakespeare - 'The better part of valour is discretion.'

	Goldsmith - 'He who fights and runs away, may live to fight another day.'
Shuttlecock	A predecessor of modern badminton, played with rackets and a feathered 'bird.'
Spying Fan	Also known as Monocular Fans. A lady's brisé or cockade fan with a miniature spy-glass added to the rivet or centre, so that one might peep discreetly at one's surroundings.
St Giles	The Seven Dials area of central London, close to Covent Garden.
Stockade	A barrier constructed with upright wooden posts or stakes as a defence against attack.
Sugar nips	A large pair of pincers designed to cut sugar from a block or sugarloaf.
Tale-bearers are as bad as the tale-makers	As said by Mrs Candour in R B Sheridan's 'School for Scandal' (1777).
Talisman	An object (such as a rabbit's foot) thought to contain magical powers, protect from ill will and bring good luck.
Tattle	Gossip, scandal, tittle-tattle.
Teaching to fish	Proverb: 'Give a man a fish and he will eat for a day. Teach a man how to fish and you feed him for a lifetime.'

Temple of Concord and The Temple of Peace	Both located in Green Park, central London. The Temple of Peace was destroyed in 1749 during a firework display, as was the Temple of Concord in 1814, during the Prince Regent's Gala.
Timon	Darcy is referencing Shakespeare's (and possibly Thomas Middleton's) 'Timon of Athens' (1607).
Truefitt & Hill's Freshman Cologne	The world's oldest barbershop, established in 1805, St James's, London.
Whist	A common card game in Jane Austen's era, played between four players (two opposing pairs).
Wickham, Mr	The infamous rake of Pride & Prejudice; extremely charming and untruthful. He befriends Lizzy and relays a false history of his acquaintance with Mr Darcy, encouraging her prejudice towards him to develop further. Later in the novel, he seduces Lydia Bennet, exposing the Bennet family to potential ruin.
Wollstonecraft, Mary	An English writer, philosopher and advocate of women's rights; far ahead of her time. Today Wollstonecraft is considered one of the founding feminist philosophers, being best known for 'A Vindication of the Rights of Woman' (1792), in which she

argues for equality, education and imagines a social order founded on reason. (1759 - 1797)

With gratitude to: -

Jane Austen

Austen Authors

Jane Austen Centre

Jane Austen's World

Pemberley.com

Randombitsoffascination.com

Regencydances.org

The Jane Austen Wiki

Vic Sanborn

Wikipedia

'Lizzy & Darcy in Lockdown' is also available to view via YouTube on Summer Light Theatre's Channel.